Laughingly he took the tinsel from her hair

"Happy Christmas, darling," Logan said softly.

Callie looked up at him with love-filled eyes, suddenly feeling tearful, suddenly feeling too much happiness at once.

"Let's go inside," he groaned, leaning back against the closed door to pull her roughly into his arms, his mouth devouring hers with a fierce passion. "I missed you today," he murmured into her hair.

"I missed you, too." Callie trembled in his arms.

Logan's eyes darkened as he gazed down at her. "You look like a child," he muttered, smoothing the hair from her face.

She smiled at him. "But sometimes I don't act like one," she said provocatively.

"No." Logan gave a husky laugh, pulling her toward him. "You most certainly don't."

CAROLE MORTIMER
is also the author of these

Harlequin Presents

Many of these books are available at your local bookseller.

For a free catalog listing all titles currently available,
send your name and address to:

HARLEQUIN READER SERVICE
1440 South Priest Drive, Tempe, AZ 85281
Canadian address: Stratford, Ontario N5A 6W2

CAROLE MORTIMER

love's only deception

Harlequin Books

TORONTO • NEW YORK • LOS ANGELES • LONDON
AMSTERDAM • PARIS • SYDNEY • HAMBURG
STOCKHOLM • ATHENS • TOKYO • MILAN

Harlequin Presents first edition May 1983
ISBN 0-373-10594-0

Original hardcover edition published in 1983
by Mills & Boon Limited

CHAPTER ONE

CALLIE added jam to her buttered toast, knowing she would have to start getting ready soon, but lingering reluctantly over her breakfast, making herself another cup of coffee. After all, it wasn't a long drive from London to Berkshire.

She wished she didn't have to go, that Jeff hadn't put her in this position. Hadn't she gone through enough the last six months—her mother's death, Jeff's own death in a car accident, and now she had to meet his family, a family who hadn't even wanted to speak to her themselves but had contacted her through a lawyer. She had disliked James Seymour on sight.

He had sat in that dusty-looking office, surrounded by rows and rows of huge official-looking books, the whole room looking like a mausoleum. And James Seymour had been totally in keeping with the room, fusty and old, looking down his nose at her as he informed her she was the sole beneficiary of Jeff's will.

'*I* am?' she gasped. 'Oh, but surely there must be some mistake,' she protested.

James Seymour looked as if he thought so too, and that Jeff, dear kind, loving Jeff, had made it! 'I can assure you there is no mistake,' he said in his haughty voice. 'I was Mr Spencer's lawyer for many years, did in fact draw up this will for him. Caroline Day, 28, Hill Apartments, London. That is you, isn't it?'

'Well . . . yes. But I don't want any of—of that,' she pointed wildly at the will laid out in front of the lawyer.

7

He looked at her as if she were slightly deranged. 'Three-quarters of a million pounds, seven hundred and sixty-three thousand pounds, to be exact——'

'Oh, let's be exact,' she said shrilly, sure this man didn't know what he was talking about. Jeff hadn't been rich, not that rich anyway. Three-quarters of a million pounds! It was unthinkable, unimaginable.

James Seymour looked at her over the top of his glasses. 'I was being exact,' he said stiffly. 'There is also the matter of thirty-seven and a half per cent of the shares of Spencer Plastics——'

'*Spencer* Plastics?' she questioned sharply.

His mouth tightened. 'We would get on a lot quicker, Miss Day, if you would refrain from constantly interrupting me.'

'Yes, but *Spencer* Plastics? Sorry,' she mumbled at his quelling look, the eyes behind the gold-rimmed glasses the cold grey of the sea on a winter's day.

Had she gone mad? She had looked warily at the letter when it had arrived last week, should have guessed there was something wrong when she had telephoned the office of Seymour, Seymour, Seymour, and Brown, and they had refused to divulge the reason for requesting to see her over the telephone.

'If we could continue?' James Seymour said woodenly.

'Go ahead. I mean—please do,' she blushed at his condescending look.

'Mr Spencer, Mr Jeffrey Spencer, that is, left you his shares in the family company——'

'You mean Jeff—I mean Jeffrey, was related to the Spencers of Spencer Plastics?' Even she had heard of the powerful Spencer family, Sir Charles and Lady Spencer, and Sir Charles' sister Cicely. But surely the

Charles and Cissy Jeff had sometimes spoken of couldn't be them . . .?

'Jeffrey Spencer was Sir Charles' younger brother,' she was informed distantly.

It was what she had already guessed, what she had dreaded him confirming. Jeff had never said, never given any indication—Dear God, that family would eat her alive if she dared to claim those shares!

'I—Do they know about me?' she asked nervously.

'I believe Mr Spencer told them of your relationship, yes.'

'No, not that. I mean, do they know about Jeff's will?'

'Yes, they know.'

Oh, lord! They were probably ready to lynch her from the highest tree by now. The Spencer family was one of the most powerful in the world of plastics, and they would hardly welcome a little nobody like her into their midst. If only Jeff had told her who his family was, explained to her what he meant to do!

'Sir Charles has expressed a wish to see you,' the lawyer told her now.

She would just bet he had, and she could guess what about. 'When?' she asked dully.

'This weekend, if that's possible.'

It didn't sound as if she had much choice. 'I—Well, yes, I suppose so.'

'Good. Sir Charles is expecting you.' He handed her a piece of his official-looking notepaper with Sir Charles' address on. 'For the weekend,' he added firmly.

Callie's eyes widened, deep brown eyes with golden flecks in their depths. Her hair was the colour of corn, straw-coloured she called it, straight and thick to just below her shoulders, the full fringe shaped about her small heart-shaped face, making her eyes the dominant feature, her nose small and short, her mouth wide and smiling—usually—her figure petite, even boyish, and at twenty-two years of age she had given up the idea of growing any taller than her five feet two inches in height.

'For the weekend . . .?' she echoed weakly.

'Yes. Sir Charles feels it would be advisable for you to meet the family. I understand the nephew will not be there,' James Seymour's voice cooled perceptively, giving Callie the impression that he disliked the absent nephew even more than he apparently disliked her—if that were possible. His disdain for her had been obvious from the moment she had entered the office half an hour earlier. 'I believe business matters have taken him out of the country,' he explained abruptly.

Callie could understand his reluctance to talk to her—after all, she had no real claim on the Spencer family, and James Seymour obviously thought so too, revealing the family movements as if pressured to.

Well she had had enough, she didn't want to hear any more. 'Please tell Sir Charles I accept his invitation. I have to leave now——'

'We haven't finished, Miss Day——'

'I'm sorry,' she stood up, 'but I really do have to go. Perhaps you could send me a letter explaining everything in more detail?' she added to soften the blow.

He looked as if she had insulted him, sitting ramrod-straight in the leather desk-chair. 'That isn't the way I like to do business, Miss Day——'

'Well, I'm sorry, but I have to go. I'll call you,' she told him before disappearing out of the door.

It all seemed like a bad dream, the money, the thirty-seven and a half per cent shares in Spencer Plastics. She felt sure she would wake up soon and just be ordinary Callie Day with none of the responsibility of money and shares.

She told her friend Marilyn so; Marilyn and her husband Bill lived in the flat next door. 'I'm sure the haughty Mr Seymour will find there's been some mistake. He has to,' she groaned.

Marilyn shook her head dazedly. 'I don't know what you're complaining about. You're rich, don't you realise that?'

'Of course I do,' Callie frowned. 'Although Mr Seymour said it would take several months to sort out the details. But I don't feel I have any right to those things.'

'Jeff wanted you to have them, that's all the right you need.'

'I doubt the Spencer family see it that way,' she grimaced.

The two of them were sitting in Marilyn's kitchen drinking tea, baby Paul playing happily at their feet.

'From what I can tell, you're more Jeff's family than any of that snobby lot,' commented Marilyn. 'Not one of them came to the funeral.'

Callie shrugged. 'Mr Seymour said they weren't informed in time. Anyway, I wouldn't have wanted them there,' she added with a catch in her throat. 'Only people who loved you while you were alive should be allowed to say goodbye to you. Jeff always said that.'

'And now Jeff is saying he wants you to have those things, that he still wants to take care of you,' Marilyn pointed out gently. 'If you turn them down it will be like throwing his love back in his face.'

. Put like that, she had little choice but to go to Berkshire for this weekend, grit her teeth and make the most of it. But she felt sure it was going to be a disaster.

She got up from the breakfast table, if it could be called that at eleven-thirty in the morning! Sir Charles and Lady Spencer would probably be scandalised by such behaviour. But she had been out with some friends the evening before, a party that had gone on long into the early hours of this morning, carrying on to one of the girls' flats once the other party had ended. Her hangover wasn't going to help her cope with the Spencer family! She was expected for dinner, Mr Seymour had told her when she telephoned his office yesterday, his manner even more frosty than at their first meeting.

A long soak in the bath, her hair washed, and she was starting to feel a little more human, although what to wear was another problem. She was invited to dinner, and yet she would be arriving late afternoon. Of course she could always change before dinner . . . Yes, that was what she would do, what she would be *expected* to do. Oh dear, she was going to make a fool of herself this weekend, she just knew she was. She wasn't used to mixing with Sirs and Ladies, and she usually sat down to dinner in whatever she had worn to the office that day!

She chose one of the suits she wore to work to arrive in, a black tailored skirt and jacket, a white Victorian-style blouse worn beneath the jacket, a large cameo brooch pinned at her throat. Her hair swung smoothly about her shoulders, clean and silky, her whole appearance was one of cool confidence. She just hoped she acted that way when she got there.

Once she got out of London and on to the motorway it was a clear run down to Berkshire, her ten-year-old Ford Escort excelling itself and doing a steady sixty miles an hour. Royal Berkshire, the home of Windsor Castle, one of the Queen's residences. It was also the home of the Windsor Safari Park, which perhaps wasn't quite so prestigious. Maybe that was one of the subjects she should avoid this weekend.

The trouble was she had no idea what she was going to talk about! They obviously couldn't discuss Jeff and the shares for the whole of the time she was there, and she doubted she would have anything else in common with the Spencer family. The truth of the matter was, she had nothing in common with them, not even Jeff. He had been as far removed from them as she was, hadn't even owned to being a member of the family.

Dear Jeff. Callie had loved him so much, his death had come as a shock to her, even more so than her mother's, which had been expected, as her illness had been terminal. But the car accident that had taken Jeff from her too had left her numbed with grief, still had the power to reduce her to tears, and she rapidly blinked them away as she saw the turn-off for Ascot.

She had instructions to the Spencer house from there; the name of the house did not reveal its location. She followed the instructions implicitly, and finally found herself completely out in the country, slowly turning the Escort down a long gravel driveway, a huge stately Tudor manor house standing at the end of it.

The gardens were resplendent with flowers, despite the lateness of the season, the October weather not being exactly conducive to the delicate blooms.

Someone obviously tended these gardens with tender loving care—and why not? she thought cynically. Money could achieve most things, even a flowering garden in October. Oh dear, she *was* getting cynical! But maybe that was the only way she was going to get through this weekend. Sir Charles was likely to eat her alive otherwise.

Her Escort looked slightly out of place next to the Jaguar, a Rolls-Royce parked next to it, a huge garage at the side of the house containing two more cars, although from this distance she couldn't tell their make.

There was a man coming down the steps towards her as she got out of her car, a tall grey-haired man of perhaps fifty, fifty-five, still handsome despite his years, the superb cut of his cream trousers and Norfolk jacket pointing to him not being a servant. Could this possibly be Sir Charles himself?

Callie closed her eyes. Oh Jeff, Jeff—she was in the lions' den now, and he had put her there.

She didn't fit in with these people, should never have come here. Just the house was enough to frighten the life out of her! It was certainly nothing like the small flat Jeff had shared with her for the last four years.

The man she assumed to be Sir Charles Spencer looked no more welcoming than the house did, seeming slightly surprised by her. 'Miss Day . . .?' He looked at her with narrowed blue eyes.

She put her overnight case down on the gravel and slammed the boot shut, hoping it wouldn't shoot up again as it often did. It didn't and she gave a relieved smile as she straightened. 'Yes, I'm Caroline Day,' she confirmed breathlessly.

'Charles Spencer.' He thrust his hand out at her.

'I'm pleased to—meet you,' she faltered in her warm greeting as he barely touched her hand before releasing it again.

'Come into the house.' He didn't return her polite greeting, but bent to pick up her small suitcase. Suddenly he frowned. 'I had no idea you were so—young,' he said bluntly.

Callie held herself back from saying she hadn't realised he was so old! 'I'm twenty-two,' she felt she almost had to defend herself.

'My dear, in my book that is young.'

Maybe it was to a man of fifty, but plenty of her friends were already married with children of their own. 'Jeff always said——'

'Jeff?' Sir Charles pounced. 'Do you mean my brother Jeffrey?'

'Er—yes. He always said that you're only as young, or old, as you feel.'

His mouth twisted contemptuously. 'Looking at you, Jeffrey must have felt very young indeed,' he drawled.

She didn't like this man, not his manner towards her, or his derogatory way of talking about Jeff. No matter what their differences, and from Sir Charles' manner there had to have been a lot, Jeff had never made a single criticism of his brother. Jeff had only ever talked of the good times, of the times when he, Charles, and Cicely were all children.

'He was always lots of fun,' she said stiffly, walking through the door the manservant held open for her.

'Take this upstairs to Miss Day's room,' Sir Charles handed her case over as if it had stung him. 'Come through to the drawing-room, Miss Day, and meet my wife and son.' He strode forward, pushing open the double oak doors.

So the nephew was here after all. If he was as pompous as his father then this was going to be a really fun weekend!

A woman stood up as they entered the room, or rather, she flowed up, moving with a liquid grace that drew attention to the perfection of her tall figure. She was a beautiful woman, although obviously of middle age, her black hair perfectly coiffured, her beautiful face made up in dark and light shades that gave her an ageless appearance. The grey silk dress she wore looked as if it were real silk. Thank goodness, Callie thought, she had put on something smart herself!

'My wife Susan,' Sir Charles introduced needlessly. 'Susan, this is Miss Day.'

Lady Spencer's handshake was as fleeting as her husband's had been, her slender fingers barely touching Callie's. And had it been her imagination, or had Sir Charles emphasised the 'this' in the introduction, almost as if she weren't what they had been expecting. Maybe they just weren't used to the lower classes, they didn't either of them look as if they got off their pedestal very often. No wonder you got away from this lot, Jeff, Callie thought ruefully. They would have suffocated him with their stuffy attitudes and falsely polite manners.

'Please call me Callie,' she invited, not one to stand on ceremony, even if they were. 'Everyone does.'

'Including—Jeff?' Sir Charles drawled.

She flushed, although she had no idea why. 'He never called me anything else.'

'But your name is Caroline, isn't it?' Lady Spencer spoke for the first time, her accent so terribly-terribly

English that Callie's eyes widened. She hadn't thought anyone really spoke like *that*.

'Yes, it's Caroline. But——'

'Then that is what we will call you,' Lady Spencer said dismissively.

Whether you like it or not, Callie thought resignedly. 'As you wish,' she shrugged.

'Would you care for tea?' the other woman asked languidly.

'Oh—er—yes. Tea would be lovely.'

She occupied herself with looking around the room while Lady Spencer rang for the tea, guessing the paintings on the wall to be originals, the antique furniture and ornaments all genuine too. The room was exactly what television and films always portrayed for the English gentry, and to Callie it was all like being in some terrible play, with her as the main character, ignorant of the roles of her fellow-actors.

'Donald is in the study taking a telephone call,' Lady Susan said in answer to her husband's question.

Sir Charles' face darkened. 'I'll go and get him.'

Callie was curious about Donald Spencer, wondering what was so terrible about him that James Seymour disliked him. Maybe he grew his hair too long, that was sure to annoy the balding lawyer.

'Jeffrey was alone in the car at the time of the accident, I believe,' Lady Spencer interrupted her thoughts.

Pain flickered across her face before she could control it. 'Yes, he was alone.' Fun-loving Jeff, who was never alone, who hated to be alone, had been trapped in his car for over an hour before he died; the rescuers had been unable to get to him in time to save him, and his chest had been crushed so badly that he died in anguish. Callie shuddered with the horror of it. The way Jeff had died often came back to haunt her in horrific nightmares. 'All alone,' she repeated harshly.

'I——'

The doors swung open and Sir Charles came in, a younger version of himself at his side. Callie looked at Donald Spencer with interest, seeing the youthful handsomeness that had once been Sir Charles', the only difference being that Donald's hair was as fair as her own, and there was perhaps a certain weakness about the chin that wasn't present in the father.

But neither of these men bore any resemblance to Jeff, Jeff of the laughing blue eyes, the unruly dark hair, denims and a casual shirt his usual attire.

Donald Spencer was dressed as formally as his father, and he looked as if he were never dressed any other way. Did no one ever relax in this family?

'This is my son Donald,' Sir Charles told her needlessly.

A frown creased her brow. Why was it she had the feeling there should have been a fanfare attached to that announcement?

Donald was looking at her with stunned eyes. 'You aren't what I was expecting,' he blurted out, and received a scowl from his father, a warning look from his mother, and a ruddy hue coloured his cheeks as he muttered an apology.

So she had been right about the weakness about the chin. Donald Spencer was nowhere near as self-confident as his parents. She instantly felt a sympathy for him. 'You aren't what I was expecting either,' she smiled.

'Did Uncle Jeffrey talk about us, then?' he wanted to know.

How could she say never? She had had no idea Jeff even had a nephew, let alone who Charlie was. How Sir Charles must have hated being called that. And how Jeff would have loved to taunt him with it! Jeff had loved to tease, had a warped sense of humour that she shared, a sense of humour she hoped was going to get her through this.

'Sometimes,' she compromised.

'But you never felt impelled to meet any of his family?' once again it was Lady Spencer who asked the probing question.

Callie sensed reprimand, and bristled resentfully. 'As you never felt compelled,' she returned waspishly.

The other woman's mouth twisted mockingly. 'You are hardly family, Caroline,' she drawled insultingly.

Callie blanched, the shaft going home. 'No, I'm not, am I?' she said stiffly.

Lady Spencer looked down her haughty nose at her. 'You see, we feel——'

'Tea, my dear,' Sir Charles interrupted as the maid wheeled in the tea-trolley, almost thankful for the interruption, it appeared to Callie.

'Please sit down, Miss Day,' Lady Spencer invited graciously as she took charge of the silver teapot. 'Cream or lemon?' she looked up to enquire.

A spark of rebellion entered Callie's eyes, the gold flecks instantly more noticeable. It was obvious that this family thought she was something rather unpleasant that had momentarily entered their lives, and that they also expected her not to even have the social graces.

'Is it fresh lemon?' she asked coldly.

Her hostess looked affronted. 'Of course.'

'Then I'll have lemon,' she accepted abruptly, moving back from her perched position on the edge of the chair to lean back against the soft leather, so that Lady Spencer had to bend forward to give her the steaming cup of tea. 'Thank you.' Her tone was still curt.

'Sandwich, Miss Day?' Donald Spencer held out a plate to her, tiny squares of bread arranged invitingly on the delicate china. 'These are salmon, and these cucumber,' he pointed out.

Of course, what else? 'Thanks.' She took two of the tiny sandwiches, wondering if she was actually supposed to eat them. No one really lived like this, did they? It was so unreal, so—so pompous.

'We were talking about the accident, Caroline.' Lady Spencer spoke again, looking at her enquiringly from beneath arched brows as Callie choked on her sandwich. 'Donald, pat her on the back—gently!' she instructed after the first painful thump landed in the middle of Callie's back.

'I'm all right,' she choked as Donald went to hit her again, sitting on the arm of her chair to do so. She blinked back the tears and swallowed hard. 'Sorry,' she mumbled.

Lady Spencer nodded regally. 'Donald, don't sit on the arm of the chair like that,' she said waspishly.

He at once moved back to his own armchair. Just like an obedient child, Callie thought with a shake of her head. Donald must be about thirty, his late twenties at least, and yet he still seemed to live here with his parents, something she found unbelievable for a man. Perhaps he had a home of his own in London, was only here for the weekend as she was, although she doubted it. Donald had the look of a devoted son, too much so in her opinion.

It had been the mention of Jeff's accident that had

sparked off her choking and coughing fit. Why did this woman persist in talking about it? Jeff was dead, no amount of talking could bring him back, as could no amount of crying, although when she was alone she couldn't seem to stop the latter.

Her head went back, her chin held at a proud angle. '*We* weren't talking about the accident, Lady Spencer,' she said distantly, 'you were. I really have nothing to say about it. Jeff is dead, that's all there is to say.'

'Jeff is Jeffrey,' Sir Charles told his family dryly.

Callie's eyes flashed. 'I never knew him as anything other than Jeff.'

'Of course you didn't, my dear,' he soothed. 'Perhaps you would like to go to your room and rest, you look a little pale.'

'The mourning colour always does that to blondes, darling,' his wife told him in a bored voice.

Callie flushed. 'I didn't wear this suit because I'm in mourning.'

'Of course you didn't,' Lady Spencer said tartly. 'We would hardly expect you to mourn for Jeffrey. He's left you a very rich young woman, why should you mourn him?'

'Susan——'

'Perhaps I should go to my room.' Callie stood up jerkily. 'If you'll excuse me . . .'

'Donald, take Miss Day up to her room,' Lady Spencer commanded irrritably.

'Of course.' He stood obediently to his feet, moving to open the door for her.

Callie walked out without saying another word. She had expected opposition, even resentment from this family, but she hadn't expected open dislike. But why hadn't she? She was an intruder, a usurper. James Seymour had explained that the other sixty-two and a half per cent of Spencer Plastics was owned by the family—and Lady Spencer had already told her that she certainly wasn't that!

'Mother doesn't always mean things the way they sound,' Donald spoke suddenly at her side, more relaxed now that he was away from his parents' domination.

Callie looked at him with new eyes, seeing the rather pleasant features, the friendly blue eyes. And away from his parents he didn't seem weak at all, his lighter personality was no longer overshadowed by them.

But he didn't know his mother very well if he really didn't think she had meant that remark about Jeff leaving her a rich young woman. She was under no such illusions about Lady Spencer, she had meant every word *exactly* as it had been said—bitchily!

But the truth couldn't be denied, Jeff had left her very rich—if she dared to accept what James Seymour had told her about Jeff's will. Up until today she really hadn't thought it could be true, was sure they would find it was all a mistake, and yet now she had to believe it, the Spencers' resentment had made it so. She needed time alone to adjust to this new sensation, to accept that she really was as rich as James Seymour had said she was.

'I'm sure she doesn't,' she answered Donald blandly. 'My coming here has been—a surprise to you all.'

'Yes,' he agreed truthfully. 'It never occurred to us that Uncle Jeffrey would—Oh well, it's done now.'

'Yes,' she answered huskily. 'Yes, it's done now.'

'Oh, I didn't mean——' His cheeks flooded with

colour, made to look even worse on his normally pale cheeks.

'I'm sure you didn't,' she squeezed his arm in sympathy. 'Thank you for showing me to my room.'

He smiled. 'My pleasure,' he pushed the bedroom door open before turning to her. 'You really aren't what we were expecting, you know.'

Callie quirked an eyebrow, her curiosity aroused. 'And just what were you expecting?'

'Oh, someone older, more—more——'

'Sophisticated and money-grasping?' she finished softly, walking into the bedroom and throwing her clutch-bag down on the bed, not even sparing a glance for the beautifully furnished room she was to sleep in tonight.

'No——'

She gave a tight smile. 'I'm sorry I didn't fall into the right category, Donald. Maybe I could work at it?'

'No, please——'

'I'm sorry,' she sat down heavily on the bed. 'This meeting has been as trying for me as it has for you.' She put a hand up to her aching temple. 'Now I really would like to rest.'

He took her hint to leave. 'Dinner is at eight o'clock. Shall I call for you?'

It would mean she didn't have to walk into the midst of the lions' den on her own. 'I'd like that,' she accepted gratefully.

'Good,' he said eagerly. 'I'll see you later, then.'

Callie lay back on the bed once she was alone, staring up at the ornate ceiling. With Jeff at her side she might have got through this, alone she had no defences. But if Jeff had been alive she would never have come here, would never have been allowed through the doors! Oh, Jeff, what have you done to me? she groaned, turning her face into the pillow and crying for her loss.

She must have actually fallen asleep, for the sun was just going down when she at last opened her eyes. She sat up groggily, pushing her hair from her eyes and looking around her dazedly. The curtains were still drawn back, the last of evening's light fading. Jeff had always liked sunrise and sunset, they were his favourite times of day, and the two of them had often shared those times together.

She hadn't slept well since Jeff had died, had missed his presence in the flat, finding herself surrounded by the memories there. Maybe she should move, try to forget, and yet she had been loath to do that, to leave the memories behind. Maybe one day, when she was ready to let the memories go. But not yet, not yet . . .

Her suit was badly creased after she had slept in it, and she hung it up in the wardrobe, seeing that the dress and trousers she had brought with her were already in there, her shoes laid out neatly on the floor, the empty suitcase beside them. A search of the dressing-table drawers found her clean underwear, silky pantyhose, pink lacy panties and matching bra, and she didn't like the idea of some unknown person sorting through her more intimate clothing, it was like an invasion of her privacy. She had packed and unpacked her own clothing since she had been on a school trip when she was ten years old, and she didn't like the fact that someone else had done it for her now. She had always been an independent, self-reliant person, and she doubted she would ever want that to change. Even if she was supposedly rich now! She wasn't going to let any of this change her life, and she certainly didn't intend to give up her private life to an army of servants.

Her dress was a deep, rich brown velvet, making her eyes appear the same way, giving her skin a honey-tone, the halter-neckline showing a large expanse of her flesh, the straight style of the skirt showing her slender curves to advantage.

When Donald knocked on the door for her she looked cool and attractive, and saw his eyes deepen in appreciation as his gaze ran from the top of her golden head to the tip of her tiny feet.

He looked very handsome himself in a black dinner suit, his shirt snowy white, his short hair brushed neatly away from his face. He really was the most innocuous-looking individual, and Callie couldn't for the life of her imagine what it was James Seymour disliked about him.

The two older members of the Spencer family were already in the lounge when she entered with Donald. Lady Spencer's peacock-blue full-length gown gave her a more regal look than before, and Sir Charles' black dinner suit was as well cut as his son's.

Dinner was a very strained affair, with the four of them making polite conversation, no mention being made of the reason Callie was here. By the end of the meal her head ached with the effort of trying to enjoy the meal and look relaxed, when all she really wanted to do was get away from here, go back to London and forget she had ever met Jeff's snooty relatives. Maybe if his sister Cissy had been here things might have been easier; Jeff had always spoken of his sister with affection.

Coffee in the lounge was even more of a strain; the conversation suddenly seemed to dry up completely.

Callie put her cup back on the silver tray. 'I—I think I'll go to bed. I have a headache,' she told them truthfully.

'Nonsense,' Lady Spencer said briskly. 'Fresh air is the best cure for a headache. Donald, take Caroline for a walk in the garden.'

Her eyes widened. Being alone with Donald Spencer was the last thing she had in mind for getting rid of the throb at her temples. 'Perhaps a couple of aspirin . . .' she began.

'Not when you've been drinking wine,' the other woman dismissed. 'Fresh air, that's what you need. Donald!' she prompted her son sharply.

He looked as reluctant as Callie felt! 'I—Of course,' he agreed instantly. 'Caroline?'

'It really is too chilly an evening——'

'Get Caroline my jacket, Charles,' Lady Spencer instructed her husband.

Callie knew when she was defeated, and gave in gracefully to the dictates of her hostess. Lady Spencer appeared to her rather like a puppeteer, and when she pulled the strings they all jumped into action.

Lady Spencer's 'jacket' turned out to be a mink, and Callie felt revulsion for the article as Sir Charles slipped it about her shoulders. She had always hated the breeding and killing of animals just to provide a woman with the prestige of owning a fur coat, not even wanting to think how many mink had been killed to make up this jacket. It made her feel nauseous to wear it!

She had been right, the evening was chill, and yet as soon as she could she took the jacket from about her shoulders, preferring to carry it than feel it against her skin.

'You'll catch a chill,' Donald warned as they walked through the heavily scented rose garden at the side of the house, a single light illuminating their way.

'I'm fine.' She repressed a shiver, knowing he wouldn't understand her aversion to the coat.

'Headache going?'

He sounded as if he really cared, and she smiled at him. 'Yes, it's going,' which, miraculously, it was.

'You're very beautiful, Caroline,' he remarked suddenly.

The remark was as unexpected as it was surprising. This family, not one of them, had reason to like her, to even be polite to her, and yet Donald had gone out of his way to be nice to her. She liked him if only for that reason. 'Thank you, Donald,' she accepted huskily.

'I can't understand——' He broke off, frowning his consternation.

Callie gave a light laugh. 'Can't understand *why* you think I'm beautiful? Or is it something else you don't understand?' she looked at him curiously.

'Something else,' he muttered.

'Like what?' she teased.

'I—Did you really care for Uncle Jeffrey?'

She flushed. So they were back to the subject of Jeff and whether or not she was entitled to what he had chosen to leave her. 'Yes, I cared for him,' she said stiffly. 'Very much, as it happens.'

'You loved him?'

'There was nothing not to love,' she shrugged. 'Did you ever meet him?'

Donald shook his head. 'I was only three when he left.'

'And you've never seen any of his work?'

'Work?' Donald frowned. 'What work?'

Heavens, these people didn't know Jeff had been a sculptor, that he could bring clay alive beneath his gentle fingertips! She had always thought Jeff the most uncomplicated, giving man she had ever known, and it came as a shock to her to find he had kept secrets from everyone.

'Your uncle was Jeff Thornton.'

Donald still looked puzzled. 'Jeff who?'

Callie sighed. 'Jeff Thornton. He had a very successful exhibition of his sculptures about a year ago.' It hadn't exactly made him a fortune, as Jeff had joked, he wouldn't get rich from it, but it had given his individual talent the recognition it deserved.

The way that Jeff had struggled and slaved to get that exhibition made her respect and love for him deepen. With the money he had, his influential family, he could have commanded that exhibition. Instead he had chosen to assume a pseudonym, to get recognition on his own talent.

Donald's eyebrows rose. 'I'm sure my parents didn't know about that.'

'That he was a sculptor, or that he was successful at it?' she taunted.

He flushed at the rebuke in her voice. 'Both. I—You see, Uncle Jeffrey walked out years ago. None of us really knew what he was doing. The only contact we ever had from him was through our lawyer.'

'James Seymour?'

'You've met him, haven't you?'

'Oh yes,' she nodded. 'I've met him.' She repressed a shiver. 'Could we go back inside now?'

'Of course,' he was instantly solicitous. 'How's the headache?'

'Gone,' she lied, handing him the jacket as soon as

they were inside the house. 'Would you please excuse me to your parents, I'd like to go straight to bed.' Before she collapsed with the strain of this weekend.

'Certainly. Goodnight, Caroline.'

She returned the politeness, but she had the feeling that the night was going to be far from good. There had been too much talk of Jeff today for the nightmares not to return.

She awoke in a state of panic in the early hours of the morning, a fine sheen of perspiration on her brow, her hands clenching and unclenching at her side. God, she thought, would she ever lose the guilt, the knowledge that Jeff had been picking her up from work, as her own car was in the garage being serviced, that he wouldn't have been driving down that particular road at that particular time if it hadn't been for her.

She had waited outside her office building for over half an hour, deciding that Jeff must have become immersed in his work and forgotten about her. He often did that, and it was no hardship to her to get the bus. It was only when she arrived home and found a policeman waiting for her that she realised she wouldn't be able to tease Jeff about his bad memory, that she would never be able to tease him again . . .

She went down to breakfast the next morning pale and heavy-eyed, and the lemon trousers and blouse she wore made her appear paler than ever.

Only Donald was in the breakfast-room when she went in to have her coffee; the thought of food was unpalatable to her. He stood up to pull her chair out for her, once again wearing well-cut trousers and a contrasting Norfolk jacket. 'Mother always has breakfast in her bedroom,' he excused her absence. 'And Father is out riding.'

Callie's eyebrows rose. 'You have horses?' She could at least talk to Donald, feeling only relief at his parents' absence, knowing that they still hadn't discussed the real reason she was here, that before she left this afternoon the question of her business involvement with this family would have to be talked about in more detail. And she was dreading it, knowing their resentment was justified.

'We have stables out at the back of the house,' Donald answered her. 'You wouldn't have been able to see them yesterday when you arrived. Do you ride?'

'Only in cars,' she answered teasingly.

Donald obviously lacked a sense of humour, and took her seriously. 'Then I'll take you out for a drive this morning.'

'Oh no, really——'

'I insist. Mother won't leave her room until almost lunch-time anyway, and I have no idea when Father will be back.'

He seemed to genuinely want to take her, and so with some reluctance she agreed, going upstairs to collect her jacket before going outside to meet him. He had driven the Jaguar up in front of the house and came round to open the door for her.

Berkshire really was a beautiful county. A lot of it still owned by the Crown, and what wasn't was mainly owned by people almost as rich. Some of the houses they passed were magnificent, although the Spencers' was still the most beautiful she had seen.

They stopped for a drink in a pub, greeted by several of Donald's friends, all of them as upper-crust as Donald himself. No doubt 'Mother' wouldn't approve of anyone who wasn't, in fact Callie felt sure she wouldn't.

That was why it came as something of a surprise to her when Donald asked if he could take her out one night. 'I work for Spencer head office in town,' he explained. 'So it would be a simple matter to call for you one evening.'

'Yes, but then you would have the long drive back——'

'The family has an apartment in town, I often use it.'

Now what did she say? Donald Spencer appeared to be pleasant enough, a little insipid for her tastes, but otherwise nice. But he didn't appeal to her, blond men never had for some reason, and after living with Jeff the last four years, loving every moment of it, it was going to take a special man to interest her. Donald wasn't that man.

'I'm really not sure——'

'Just dinner, Caroline,' he encouraged, his hand covering hers.

What harm could dinner do? 'All right, Donald,' she agreed reluctantly. 'I'll leave you my number and you can call me.'

'And you'll come out with me?'

'Yes.' She looked at her wrist-watch. 'Now I think we should be getting back, I wouldn't want to upset your mother by being late for lunch.'

Callie was able to eat her lunch, the traditional roast beef and Yorkshire pudding, safe in the knowledge that in an hour or two she would be able to leave. The sooner the better as far as she was concerned. Sir Charles and Lady Spencer had been overly polite during lunch, and she knew that the talk they had brought her here for couldn't be far off.

'Perhaps Caroline would like to see the roses in the daylight, Donald,' his mother suggested once they had retired to the drawing-room.

'Would you?' he asked eagerly.

Anything to get away from his parents. 'I'll love it,' Callie nodded.

It really was a spectacular garden; many of the roses were still in bloom, their aroma heady, their colours a delight to the eye, as was their perfect shape.

Donald laughed when Callie asked if his mother tended the roses herself. 'As far as gardens go my mother is a looker, not a doer. She prefers organising garden-parties, things like that,' he added as if to make up for the slight he had given his mother.

'I'm sure——'

'Telephone, Mr Donald.' The butler had quietly appeared at their side.

A look of irritation crossed Donald's face and he turned to look down at Callie. 'I'm sorry about this, but I shouldn't be long,' he apologised.

'I'll be fine out here,' she assured him.

In fact it was a relief to be on her own. She found the Spencer family, this whole situation, completely overwhelming. Maybe if she had been given the time to think about it she might even have found a way not to come here.

After about ten minutes, when Donald still hadn't returned, she decided to go back into the house, the beauty of the garden being exhausted. As she approached the open french doors into the lounge she could hear the sound of Donald's voice, and hesitated as she realised he was still on the telephone. Then she wasn't hesitating at all, but was listening avidly; the burden of the conversation seeming to be about her!

'Because of Caroline, darling,' Donald was explaining. 'You know I don't prefer her to you. No, I don't *want* to marry her, I want to marry you, but—No, don't hang up,' he begged in a panicked voice. 'Darling, please, try to be reasonable. It just means we'll have to wait a while. Until after the divorce. Well, I know it could take years, but——'

Callie was no longer listening, but slumped down on to the garden seat. The reason Donald had been so nice to her this weekend was suddenly clear to her. They were actually intending to marry her off to him. And divorce them too!

Heavens, they must really want those shares badly. Any guilt she might have felt about Jeff leaving her the shares was now erased. People like the Spencers didn't deserve to have anything that had been Jeff's. She had come here willing to be polite to them because they were Jeff's family, might even have been prepared to arrange for Sir Charles to take the shares off her. But not now.

She knew Donald didn't have the deviousness, the intelligence to come up with an idea like this, it had to have been his parents' plan. Besides, he was in love with someone else.

He had finished on the telephone now, hanging up hastily as his mother spoke to him.

'Who was that?' she demanded sharply.

'Just a friend,' he dismissed shakily.

'Are you sure, Donald?'

'Of course I am, Mother,' he said nervously.

'And where is Caroline?'

'I left her in the garden when I came in to answer the telephone.'

'And how are things going with her?'

'Well—I hope.'

'You only hope?' his mother echoed scathingly. 'You aren't pushy enough, Donald,' she tutted. 'If she doesn't like you I don't know what your father will say—or what he will do,' she added threateningly. 'We really can't have someone like *that* at Spencer Plastics.'

'But you're intending to make her my wife!' Donald groaned.

'Only for a short time, dear,' his mother dismissed.

'But——'

'Now don't be tiresome, dear. Your father will be very pleased with you if you do this for him. And it won't be for ever. You have to admit she's prettier than you had imagined.'

'Well . . . yes. But——'

'Really, Donald, you agreed to this when we discussed it earlier in the week. Now go and get Caroline. She's been left alone too long.'

By the time Donald found her Callie had regained her composure. She was back in the rose garden so that he shouldn't realise she had overheard his telephone call and his conversation with his mother. But she was able to look at them with new eyes, to see the greed in all their faces. No wonder they hadn't wanted to discuss the shares—they didn't need to, they intended getting their hands on them when she married Donald. Whoever had thought of such an idea must have a warped mind.

And to imagine she would actually fall for Donald, that was an insult to her intelligence!

CHAPTER TWO

SHE had calmed down somewhat by the time she got home, although she was no less determined to make the Spencers pay for their cold-blooded scheme.

She persuaded Bill, Marilyn's husband, to deal with the details of her side of Jeff's will. He was a very good lawyer himself, and he wouldn't be intimidated by James Seymour or the Spencer family.

With that worry off her mind Callie's time was free to accept Donald Spencers' invitation. But if he thought she was going to be an easy conquest he was going to be out of luck. She would make sure he took her to all the most expensive places in town. The Spencer family had angered her, and Donald was going to know all about dating *Callie* Day!

He might be weak and a little stupid where his parents were concerned, but she had to admire his determination—or maybe it was just fear of his parents? Whatever the reason, Donald didn't object to anything she said or did.

And during the next month she said a lot of wild things, *did* a lot of wild things, and she made Donald do them with her, no matter how mad they were. And some of them were very extreme. She made him take off his shoes and socks one night, roll up his trousers, and paddle in the fountain with her in Trafalgar Square. Another time she took him to a really weird party, watching him squirm as an extrovert artist tried to seduce him up to her studio. And then there had been the time she made him take her to a football match, watching how awkward he felt at the disgusting language and loud behaviour of some of the rougher spectators.

Donald suffered through it all without demur, even during the modern play Callie insisted she *had* to see—even though she didn't understand a word of it! Most of it seemed to have sexual undertones, and she could see Donald becoming more and more uncomfortable by the minute, her decision to leave changed as she made him sit through it to the embarrassing end.

But nothing put him off, and by the end of four weeks she was beginning to tire of the game. The stuffy party he had brought her to tonight was the end as far as she was concerned. When he took her home she intended telling him she didn't want to see him again.

At least that way she wouldn't have to suffer through another goodnight kiss! How Donald had reached the age of twenty-eight without even learning how to kiss properly she didn't know, but somehow he had managed it, and his wet, soggy kisses were totally uninspiring.

The party was at last beginning to warm up. A lot of the older people were leaving, and the younger ones starting to let their hair down a little. Even Donald was dancing rather enthusiastically with a tall, busty blonde, for once not fawning over Callie trying to grant her every wish. When he had time to meet the girl he was really in love with she had no idea, since he had spent most of his evenings with her this last month. Perhaps one day Donald would realise there was more to life than pleasing his parents—especially at twenty-eight!

She took advantage of his preoccupation to absent herself, leaving the noisy party to go into one of the side rooms, to find herself in the peace and tranquillity of a library, its walls lined with books, books her fingers ached to touch.

She looked along the shelves, finding most of the classics, and took down her own particular favourite, leafing through the pages.

'I see I'm not the only one who needed to escape,' drawled a husky male voice.

Callie turned almost guiltily, her eyes widening as she looked at the man who had interrupted her solitude—tall, with dark, almost black hair, a rivetingly handsome face, the dark dinner suit perfectly tailored, as was the white hand-made silk shirt. She looked up into darkly grey eyes, and wondered why she hadn't noticed him at the party earlier—he was hardly the type to be overlooked.

He closed the door behind him, instantly shutting out the noise of the party, and walked across the room with long, relaxed strides, looking at the book in her hand. '*Jane Eyre*,' he mused. 'You like the story?'

His voice was deep and well modulated. 'Yes,' she blushed her confusion. 'Have you read it?'

He smiled, instantly looking younger than the mid-thirties she had guessed him to be, his teeth very white against his tanned skin, looking ruggedly attractive this close to rather than handsome. 'I think everyone should read *Jane Eyre* at least once,' he drawled.

Callie held the book in front of her almost defensively, something about this man warning her he was dangerous. 'Which means you have?' she persisted.

'Twice, actually.'

'So you liked it.'

'I think Rochester could have been a little kinder to Jane.' He shrugged. 'But if he had been perhaps she wouldn't have fallen for him. You women are reputed to fall for the bastards of life.'

Callie flushed her resentment of such a generalisation. 'We can't pick and choose whom we love—neither men nor women. And Mr Rochester wasn't kind to Jane because he was conscious of his mad wife.'

The man sat down in one of the armchairs, looking very relaxed. 'If he had been that conscious of her he would have sent her away as soon as he realised he was becoming attracted to her.'

Her mouth twisted. 'Unfortunately most humans aren't that self-sacrificing.'

He eyed her curiously for several seconds, obviously liking what he saw. 'Before we come to blows perhaps I should introduce myself. I'm Logan Carrington,' he introduced softly.

'Callie Day,' she returned stiffly.

'I've upset you,' he said ruefully. 'I didn't mean to. *Jane Eyre* is a favourite of yours, hmm?'

'Yes.' She sighed, beginning to smile at her intensity. 'Sorry,' she shrugged, 'they say you should never get into a discussion about religion or politics, but with me it's books. Everyone gets something different out of them.'

'Truce?'

'Truce.' She smiled openly now, very attractive in a dress the brown of her eyes, her hair made to look even blonder against its dark colour.

He sat forward to put his hand out to her. 'Friends?'

She hesitated for only a fraction of a second before

placing her hand in his. 'Friends,' she agreed huskily.

The touch of his hand against hers was only fleeting, and yet her fingers seemed to tingle from the contact before she hastily thrust her hand behind her back and placed the book back on the shelf. She turned to find him still watching her.

'Do I have a smut on my nose or something?' she challenged, not being used to being stared at in this way.

Logan Carrington smiled, his eyes crinkling at the corners. 'Nothing like that,' he shook his head. 'I was just wondering why a beautiful girl like you would shut herself away in here when the party is out there.'

'Maybe for the same reason you've come in here,' she returned, a glow coming to her cheeks at being called beautiful.

'I doubt it,' he grimaced. 'Unless you have secretary trouble?'

'No,' she laughed. 'I *am* a secretary.'

Much to Marilyn's disgust she had kept on with her job, sure that the bubble of her sudden wealth would burst and leave her penniless. She could do without being jobless too. She had been brought up with a sense of values, of having to work for what she had, and it was going to take months, not weeks, to accept that she no longer had to work. Besides, the question of Jeff's will hadn't been settled yet, and she didn't intend spending money she didn't even have.

'You are?' Logan Carrington looked interested.

'And very happily employed, thank you,' she told him hastily.

'Oh.'

'If your girl is incompetent——'

'She isn't,' he made a face. 'She's very good at the job.'

Callie sat down, looking puzzled. 'Then I don't understand your problem.'

'She's new, my last secretary has left to have a baby. Her replacement is—well, she—she just isn't suitable.'

The uncomfortableness of his expression told a story in itself. 'She's attracted to you,' Callie guessed with amusement.

'Yes,' he admitted with a grimace.

She had trouble holding back a smile. 'I wouldn't have thought that a drawback.'

'Except that I don't get involved with my secretaries.'

'Ah, now that is a problem.'

His eyes narrowed. 'Are you mocking me?'

'Me?' she gave him an innocently wide-eyed look. 'Of course not.'

'You are,' he gave a reluctant smile.

'Yes,' she smiled back.

'So tell me, why are you hiding in here?'

'I'm not hiding!' She was irritated by his choice of word. 'But I am bored and—and tired.'

'Tired?' He raised one dark eyebrow.

'I haven't been sleeping very well lately—and not for the reason you're thinking,' she added sharply at his speculative look. 'Do you have any idea of the pain babies suffer while they're teething?' she attacked.

'Your baby?'

'Of course not! I'm not married.'

His brows rose. 'I didn't think that was compulsory nowadays.'

'In my book it is,' Callie told him waspishly. 'The baby lives next door. And he's going through agony.'

Poor Marilyn had been pacing the floor day and night with Paul the last few weeks, and it was starting to tell on her, dark circles appearing under her eyes. And Callie knew she didn't look much better. The walls of the flat were not exactly soundproof, although not for anything would she let Marilyn and Bill know of her own disturbed nights.

'I thought they had creams and things for that nowadays,' Logan Carrington spoke now.

Her eyes widened. 'They do. But I have to admit to being surprised that you know about things like that. Do you have children of your own?'

'I'm not married,' he gave her own answer.

Well, at least she wasn't lightly flirting with a married man! 'Neices and nephews, then?'

He shook his head. 'I'm an only child. But I told you my secretary left to have a baby.'

'And she told you about teething creams?' It seemed a strange subject to discuss with one's boss.

He grinned. 'Only when I teased her about all the sleepless nights she was going to have.'

'Typical male!' Callie tried to sound annoyed, and knew she had failed miserably as Logan began to chuckle. 'I'll have you know your attitude is chauvinistic,' she added crossly.

'Yes.'

'Do you have to sound so—so proud of it?'

'Are you a Woman's Libber?'

He made it sound like something insulting, and Callie wished she could have said yes. 'No,' she admitted grudgingly. 'I admit to liking equal opportunities, but I like to be treated as a woman.'

'Protected?'

'I suppose so,' she nodded.

'You want it all ways,' he drawled mockingly.

'Yes!' her eyes flashed.

'As a man, I can tell you we like to protect. I also like a woman to have a mind of her own. We humans are a mass of contradictions, aren't we?'

'We've also discussed some very unusual subjects for two people that just met!' Callie had suddenly realised the strangeness of the situation. She and Logan Carrington had only met fifteen minutes ago, and yet they had been talking, arguing, like old friends. He was a man she found it easy to talk to, and she was aware of talking to him as she and Jeff used to talk, lightly arguing, airing different points of view. After four months it felt good to be with someone she could be like this with.

'Maybe we could discuss some more unusual subjects,' Logan suggested huskily. 'Maybe over dinner one night in the week?'

She was tempted—oh, how she was tempted! But she didn't know this man, no matter how relaxed she felt with him. She knew nothing about him except that she liked talking to him, liked the challenge of their conversation.

'I'd really like it, Callie,' he prompted.

She stood up. 'I should get back to the party.'

Logan stood up too, suddenly very serious, his expression intent. 'Dinner, Callie. Please?'

He didn't look as if it were a word that came easily to him. 'Maybe you could call me . . .'

'Give me your number,' he nodded.

She watched while he wrote it down, the pen he used obviously gold. He looked as if he might be a wealthy man; he had an air about him that spoke of authority.

She gave him the number, not really expecting to

hear from him again, sure that he wouldn't even remember the meeting tomorrow, then watched as he moved across the outer room with lithe grace to join a tall willowy redhead, whispering something in the woman's ear before they made their excuses and left. The woman had been beautiful, and their relationship was obviously intimate. No, Logan Carrington wouldn't remember her tomorrow—but Callie knew she would remember him!

'There you are!' Donald pounced. 'I've been looking for you.'

'I think I'd like to leave now, Donald,' she told him coolly.

'That's why I've been looking for you. It's late, I have to work in the morning.'

What a husband he would make! 'No, I can't make love to you tonight, I have to go to work in the morning'! He didn't know the meaning of the word spontaneity.

As she had known, he didn't take the news that she didn't want to see him again very well. But she didn't tell him the real reason she had been stringing him on this last month—let the Spencers stew for a while! Bill was looking into Spencer Plastics for her, and by the time she attended the shareholder's meeting next month she should have a fair idea of what was going on. She would knock down their marriage plans at the same time.

The telephone was ringing as she let herself into the flat, and she rushed to pick it up, the silence from the adjoining flat telling her that so far Marilyn was having an undisturbed night.

'Yes?' she hissed into the receiver.

'Callie?'

She instantly recognised the voice. 'Heavens, Logan, it's almost one o'clock in the morning!'

'Am I disturbing you?' His voice had cooled.

'I just told you, it's almost one o'clock in the——'

'I meant, are you alone?'

'Of course I—Logan!' She was indignant as she realised what he was implying.

'Ssh, you'll wake the neighbours,' he chided mockingly.

'I should think you've already done that,' she snapped, although there was still no sound from next door.

'You told me to call you——'

'Yes. But I didn't mean now, tonight——'

' "Never put off until tomorrow what you can do——" '

' "Today",' she finished the quote dryly. 'What happened to your friend?'

'Danielle?'

'If that's her name, yes.'

'As far as I know she's at home safely tucked up in bed,' he taunted.

'And why aren't you with her?'

'What makes you think I'm not?'

'I—Are you?' She blushed, even though he couldn't see her reaction to his teasing.

'No,' he chuckled. 'Believe me, she wouldn't let me call another woman while I was in her bed! And what about your partner for the evening, where's he?'

'On his way home to be safely tucked up in bed, I should think,' Callie answered mischievously.

'And why isn't he with you?'

'Because I always sleep alone,' she told him waspishly.

'Always?'

'Yes!'

'But you don't always *eat* alone?'

'No . . .'

'Dinner tomorrow, then?'

It was like being taken along in the path of a tidal wave, and Callie rebelled at this management of her life. 'Not tomorrow,' she refused. 'I already have a date,' she invented.

'Break it.'

'I most certainly will not!'

'The neighbours, Callie,' he once again taunted.

'Damn the neighbours——'

'Tut, tut, tut, you swear too.'

'Too?' she echoed sharply.

'As well as talk to strange men at parties,' he mocked.

'As I remember it, that *strange* man spoke to me first!'

'Touché,' he chuckled. 'How about dinner on Monday?'

'I——'

'Tuesday?'

I——'

'Wednesday?'

'I was about to say Monday would be fine,' she put in quickly before he got to Thursday, deciding that Monday didn't seem *too* eager. 'Although your calendar seems to be very empty for such a——' she broke off as she realised what she had been about to say. Logan Carrington needed no extra boosts to his ego from her!

'Such a . . .?' he prompted softly.

'Such a *conceited* man,' she snapped.

He chuckled. 'Tell me your address, Callie, and I'll let you get to bed.'

She told him, wondering if he rushed all his women like this. She was beginning to feel decidedly overwhelmed. So much for him forgetting all about her!

Marilyn and Bill spent the day at Bill's mother's the next day, so Callie didn't get chance to discuss Logan Carrington with her friend. She didn't quite know how to explain him to herself, she just knew she had been instantly attracted. And after Donald's inane conversation for a month it would be nice to talk to someone who obviously read as much as she did, a man of high intelligence who amused and challenged her at the same time.

In some ways he reminded her of Jeff, and yet she knew it was a mistake to compare the two men. Jeff had been very special in her life, a man with a quick intelligence and biting wit, a man who would always have a special place in her heart.

She was late home on Monday night because she went to the shops after work to get herself a new dress for her dinner-date, suddenly deciding she didn't have anything to wear. Her hair had been newly trimmed and washed at lunchtime, although she wasn't sure why she was going to so much trouble for Logan Carrington. Maybe it was because of the impeccable appearance of the beautiful Danielle. Whatever the reason, the new black dress gave her a mature sophistication.

But she forgot all about the new dress when she got back to the flat, forgot about everything but Marilyn's ashen face and Bill's stricken one.

Bill came to the door as soon as he heard her put her key in the lock. 'Could you come and talk to Marilyn?' he requested agitatedly. 'I have a couple of calls to make, and I'd rather she didn't hear them. Just in case . . .'

Callie was at once concerned. 'What's happened? Paul . . .?' she choked.

'He's fine,' Bill reassured her. 'But Marilyn's father has had a stroke. It's touch and go whether he'll make it.'

'Oh no!'

'Afraid so,' he sighed. 'Her mother called a few minutes ago, but she was pretty incoherent. I want to call the hospital myself, maybe talk to the doctor.'

'Of course.' Callie left the box containing her new dress uncaringly inside her flat, and followed Bill. 'Oh, Marilyn!' She pulled the other girl into her arms, holding her comfortingly as she began to cry.

'At least that's an improvement,' said Bill with obvious relief. 'She's just been sitting there since her mother called.'

'Shock,' Callie nodded.

'I'll be in the bedroom if you need me,' he told her pointedly.

'Oh, Callie, Callie!' Marilyn sobbed. 'He's only fifty-three, that isn't old.'

'He isn't going to die,' Callie soothed. 'Lots of people recover from strokes.'

'But they happen in threes,' her friend said hysterically. 'First your mother, then Jeff, and now——'

'He isn't going to die, Marilyn,' Callie repeated firmly, looking up as Bill came back into the room. 'What news?' she asked softly. Marilyn was crying quietly now.

'The doctor said that if he can make it through the night he'll probably be okay.'

'Only probably?' his wife choked.

'He can't make any promises, love.' Bill sat down beside her. 'No doctor could.'

'I have to go to him. I have to be with him!' She stood up, her movements agitated.

Callie touched Bill's arm. 'Go with her.'

'Paul . . .?'

'I'll take care of Paul. Stay as long as you have to.'

A look of gratitude washed over his face. 'I—I don't know how to thank you.'

'Just take care of Marilyn,' she said huskily.

It wasn't until she had fed and bathed Paul and put him to bed that she remembered her date with Logan Carrington. Well, she couldn't go anywhere now; she didn't know when she would be able to either.

But she couldn't find Logan Carrington's number in the telephone book, which meant he had an unlisted number. She couldn't let him know their date was off. He was going to turn up here at eight o'clock, and she was going to have to turn him away!

CHAPTER THREE

EXACTLY at eight o'clock Callie heard her doorbell ring, and stopped her pacing to run out to the corridor.

Logan turned from pressing her doorbell a second time, frowning as he looked at the denims and jumper she had hurriedly changed into before giving Paul his bath, knowing from experience that she would end up soaking wet too. 'I thought you lived at number twenty-eight,' he said slowly.

'I did—I mean, I do! Oh, Logan, I'm afraid our date is off for tonight!' Goodness, no wonder she was stuttering, with him looking the way he did! He should be on a danger list for women, should have a sign on him warning women to beware of him.

He was wearing a burgundy-coloured velvet jacket, a snowy white shirt, and meticulously creased black trousers, his over-long hair brushed back from his face in a fashionably windswept style. He looked over-whelming—and perhaps it was as well that their date was off for this evening. Logan was looking lethal!

His eyes narrowed to grey slits. 'Why?'

'I have to look after Paul. You see, he——'

'Invite me in, Callie,' he interrupted mockingly, 'and then you can tell me all about it.'

Before she was aware of what was happening Logan was in Marilyn and Bill's flat and she was telling him all about Marilyn's father and how she wasn't even sure when they would be back.

'Have you called the hospital?' he asked when she had finished.

She nodded. 'I spoke to Bill. He said there was no change.'

'Well, it's early yet,' Logan dismissed. 'Have you eaten?'

'No, I haven't had time. You see, Paul hadn't been fed, and——'

'Are you hungry?' he interrupted with amusement.

'Ravenous!' she admitted ruefully, having missed lunch in favour of going to the hairdressers.

'Then I don't see why we shouldn't have dinner——'

'But I just told you——'

'Here,' he finished with a raise of his eyebrows. 'Can you?'

'No, I suppose not,' she frowned. 'I have some chops in my flat, and——'

'My dear Callie, I wasn't suggesting you cook for me. You sound as if you have your hands full already. I'll send out for the food. We were going to Roberto's, I don't see any reason why he can't bring it up here.'

Callie could! Roberto's was one of the most fashionable restaurants in London, certainly not the sort of place that did take-out food! 'I don't mind cooking——'

'I won't hear of it,' he refused firmly.

'And I won't hear of you sending to Roberto's,' she said stubbornly. 'I'd rather have a Chinese.'

'You would?'

'Mm,' she smiled at his surprise. 'And there's one just two doors down from the block of flats.'

'How convenient,' he drawled. 'And I suppose I have to go down for it?'

'If it wouldn't be too much trouble,' she said with saccharin sweetness.

Logan smiled. 'Not at all.' He stood up smoothly, and the flat at once looked smaller. 'I happen to like Chinese food too.'

'How nice!'

'Callie . . .'

'Mm?' She looked up irritably.

'Would you rather I left?' he asked softly.

The evening and night stretched out in front of her like black emptiness, and she knew that being alone was the last thing she wanted. She hated everything to do with illness since her mother had died, and she was dreading Bill's next telephone call, fearing the worst.

'No,' she admitted huskily.

'I'm glad,' Logan said throatily. 'Walk me to the door?'

Considering it was only about five steps away it was a strange request, and yet as soon as she stood up it didn't seem strange any more. Logan was moving closer to her, not the door.

'I've thought about you a lot the last couple of days,' he told her softly, and one of his hands came up to cup her chin. 'You're more beautiful than I remember,' he murmured before his lips claimed hers in a gentle, probing kiss, moving away as she responded to him.

Callie looked at him dazedly. How could he think she looked beautiful in denims and a thick blue jumper?

'I won't be long,' he said briskly. 'Do you have any preferences?'

'Sweet and sour pork,' she told him instantly.

He laughed softly. 'I like a woman who knows what she wants.'

'You do?'

'Yes,' he touched her cheek gently. 'I won't be long.'

She knew he wouldn't be either. She and Jeff had food from that restaurant often, and their service was very quick. She took advantage of Logan's absence to hurry over to her flat, at least changing the jumper for a silky rust-coloured blouse, which at once made her feel less drab, adding a light make-up and lip-gloss too.

She only just managed to get back to the other flat before Logan returned, and his eyes widened appreciatively as he took in her changed appearance. Callie ignored that look, and took the bag from him to begin laying out the silver trays on the table, taking out the two plates she had put in the warmer.

Logan took off his jacket, and the white shirt stretched tautly across his wide shoulders and tapered waist.

Callie hastily averted her gaze from his powerful physique. 'Here, let me,' she held out her arms for the jacket. 'I'll hang it up.'

'Thanks,' he handed the jacket over.

His hand touched hers as she took the jacket, and Callie moved hastily away, blushing as she saw his frowning puzzlement.

They ate in silence; Logan had bought a bottle of wine to accompany their meal. Callie had to smile; she was sure this was the last way Logan had intended spending the evening.

'Care to let me in on the joke?'

She looked up to find that Logan had finished his meal and was now relaxing back in his chair, watching her intently. She bit her lip. 'It wasn't really a joke,' she said awkwardly.

'Oh?'

She blushed. 'I—I was just wondering when you last spent an evening like this.'

He stiffened. 'I don't spend all my life eating in expensive restaurants.'

Her amusement had annoyed him, she could tell that. 'I'm sorry, I—Paul!' she exclaimed in dismay as the baby let out an agonised yell. 'Excuse me,' and she hurried from the room.

The little boy was standing up in his cot crying for all he was worth, his cherubic face creased up as the tears flowed freely.

'It's all right, darling,' Callie soothed as she plucked him up into her arms, a tiny nappy-clad figure in a pair of navy blue pyjamas, his blond curls ruffled into disorder.

He didn't seem to want to stop crying, not even after she had changed his nappy and applied the soothing cream to his gums. He just kept screaming, his breath coming in short gasping sobs, and she was beginning to panic when Logan opened the nursery door.

'What's wrong?' he frowned, looking totally out of place in this baby-orientated room.

Callie gave him an angry glare. 'Well, if I knew that——'

'Okay, okay,' he cut her off tersely. 'So you don't know what's wrong with him?'

'No,' she snapped resentfully.

'Give him to me,' Logan instructed.

Her arms tightened protectively about the soft, cuddly body. 'He doesn't usually take to strangers.'

He sighed his impatience. 'I'm not going to hurt him.'

'I didn't think you were!'

'Then hand him over,' he said abruptly, his jaw rigid.

To her surprise Paul stopped crying as soon as he was in Logan's arms, his little arms going about the man's neck, his head flopping down tiredly on his shoulder.

'His teething cream will stain your shirt,' Callie whispered worriedly.

'I'll cry about it later,' he taunted.

A lump caught in her throat at the trusting way Paul was watching Logan with his big blue eyes. There was a saying about not being able to fool animals and children about a person's nature, and Paul obviously trusted Logan implicitly.

Logan was talking to the baby soothingly now— although what he was saying made Callie blush. 'So you're the one keeping Callie awake at night, hmm? I must admit I'd prefer more mature competition.'

'Logan!' she said warningly.

He chuckled softly. 'You know he doesn't understand a word.'

'No, but I do,' she blushed.

'You go and tidy up while Paul and I have a man-to-man talk,' he said with amusement.

Callie went, not wanting to hear what might be said to the baby next. What an infuriating man he was turning out to be!

To her surprise Logan quietly left the nursery about ten minutes later.

Her eyes widened. 'Asleep?'

'Asleep,' he nodded.

'How did you do it? Marilyn sometimes walks up and down with him all night, and it doesn't do any good.'

Logan sat down, stretching his long legs out in front of him. 'That's because he doesn't like being walked up and down. I sat down with him in the rocking-chair and just talked to him.'

'Oh,' she frowned her chagrin.

'Yes,' he was smiling now. 'I told him it isn't polite to interrupt another man's date with a beautiful woman, and that he would have to wait until he was older and get his own girl-friend.'

'Oh!' She was blushing now.

He shrugged. 'He understood perfectly. And now that he's asleep . . .'

She watched in trepidation as he stood up to come determinedly towards her. 'Er—Would you like dessert? I have some fresh fruit in my flat, or——'

'You,' he said softly.

'Me?' Callie gulped.

'I'd like you for dessert. Or at least,' he smiled at her expression of panic, 'a portion of you.'

She would have liked to ask which portion, but it was already too late. Logan had joined her in her armchair, and as it wasn't made to accommodate two people they were pressed very close together, Logan tenderly cupping her chin as his mouth claimed hers, gently at first, and then with increasing passion as she didn't resist him.

Callie had been waiting for him to kiss her again ever since that first probing kiss, and her arms went up about his neck as she kissed him back, her body straining against his.

He kissed her throat, the hollow between her breasts

visible by her partly unbuttoned blouse, his lips moving up to once again claim hers.

Callie felt as if she had known this man all her life, as if she had been kissed and touched by him before. And yet she hadn't, she knew practically nothing about him but his name, and it was this lack of knowledge that finally made her pull away from him, holding him at arm's length.

Logan was reluctant to release her, his grey eyes glazed with a passion that matched hers. 'Callie . . .?' he groaned, his dark hair ruffled by her fingertips, the top two buttons of his shirt undone by those same fingers.

But she hadn't been able to resist the desire to touch him, to feel the smoothness of his flesh, to touch his heated body. And Logan had liked her to touch him, had encouraged her caresses with gruff murmurs in his throat.

'I—Don't rush me,' she blushed. 'I don't even know you.'

His eyes narrowed. 'Do you need to?'

'Yes.'

'Okay,' he accepted with a sigh. 'Maybe I'd like to know more about you too. Let's get more comfortable, hmm?'

Before she was hardly aware of it Logan had shifted in the chair so that he was the only one sitting in it, with her seated on his thighs, his arms firmly about her waist.

'*This* is more comfortable?' she derided.

Logan looked up with a grin, his eyes on a level with her breasts. 'Well, isn't it?' he drawled.

'For you maybe——'

'But not for you?'

She would have liked to have said no, but the truth of the matter was it was very comfortable, and the smell of his tangy aftershave was very potent to the senses. He smelt clean and masculine, and it felt very good to sit with him like this, made her feel small and protected. But then Logan's height and breadth were such that any woman would feel this way when she was with him.

'Are you still seeing Danielle?' she probed.

Her interest in the other woman seemed to please him. 'Meaning are you one of a number?' he taunted.

'Am I?'

'No,' he smiled. 'I'm too old to cope with the intricacies of having two women in my life at the same time. I told Danielle on Saturday that I wouldn't be seeing her again.'

Callie's eyes twinkled mischievously at his description of being 'too old'. 'How old are you?' she mocked.

'Thirty five. Don't tell me, you have a rule never to go out with a man over thirty,' he groaned.

'No,' she laughed, 'I don't have a rule like that.'

'I do,' Logan told her ruefully.

Her mouth quirked teasingly. 'Never to go out with a man over thirty?'

'No, minx,' he laughed softly. 'Never to go out with a woman *under* twenty-five. And you are, aren't you?'

'Just a bit,' she nodded.

He winced. 'How much of a bit?'

'Oh—about three years,' she told him mischievously.

'Twenty-two!' he groaned, closing his eyes.

Callie frowned, seeing that it really was important to him. 'Does it bother you that much?'

He shrugged. 'It won't have to, will it?'

'But does it?'

His arms tightened about her waist. 'Not if it doesn't bother you.' It was almost a question.

'It doesn't,' she answered without hesitation.

'I was hoping you would say that.' His lips moved caressingly across her throat. 'What else would you like to know about me?'

'I'm only curious——'

'Of course. What else, Callie?'

She gave him a look of irritation for his mockery. 'Do you have any family?'

'Unfortunately, yes,' he said dryly.

'Logan!'

'Sorry, little one,' he chuckled. 'I have a mother, but she wasn't included in that "unfortunately". My uncle, aunt, and cousin were the unfortunately. My mother is a darling, although her match making has become tiresome lately,' he added with a frown.

'Maybe she would like grandchildren,' Callie blushed. There was something unsettling about discussing a man's offspring with him on a first date!

'I'm sure she would,' Logan agreed. 'But as it means I have to take a wife she's going to be disappointed.'

Her eyes widened. 'You don't intend getting married?'

He sighed, completely serious now. 'I suppose one day I'll have to.'

'*Have* to?'

'Mm. There's the family business. I'll need someone to take that over. It certainly isn't going to fall into my cousin's clutches,' he added darkly.

'You don't like him?'

'He's an idiot.'

'Logan!' she laughed her surprise at this cruelty.

'Well, he is,' he dismissed. 'He's been dominated by his parents all his life.'

Rather like Donald. 'I know what you mean,' Callie nodded her understanding.

Logan's brows rose. 'You?'

'No,' she smiled, 'just a—a friend. I had a very happy childhood, my parents were wonderful.'

'Were?'

'They're both dead now.'

'That's tough,' he commented.

'Yes. You mentioned you were in business—what business is that?'

He looked sceptical. 'You mean you don't know?'

'Of course not. I—Carrington . . .? Carrington *Cosmetics*?' she groaned.

'Right first time,' he drawled.

Callie didn't like the way he said that, almost as if she had been pretending not to know he owned the famous cosmetic company. Goodness, she probably wouldn't have spoken to him if she had known. He was *the* Logan Carrington, the playboy owner of Carrington Cosmetics. No wonder Danielle had seemed vaguely familiar—she was the girl on posters and television who advertised the newest Carrington perfume, Passion, the perfume Callie had given Marilyn for her last anniversary!

Goodness, this evening of baby-sitting and eating take-out Chinese food was even more out of character for Logan than she had realised. She struggled out of his arms and moved to the other side of the room.

Logan watched her, dark and dominating, his appearance less immaculate than when he had arrived, although no less disturbing. 'You didn't know, did you?' he said quietly.

Callie sighed. 'This may be a blow to your ego, but no, I didn't know.'

'Hell, I'm sorry, Callie. I thought——'

'You thought I was attracted to the owner of Carrington Cosmetics and not Logan Carrington the man,' she said wearily.

He stood up. 'I can see I was wrong——'

'You were!' She was angry now. 'I had a friend who told me that possessions don't make the man.'

Logan looked abashed. 'She was very astute——'

'He,' Callie corrected abruptly. 'My friend was male. And I think that tonight I've finally understood what he meant.' And she also understood *how* Jeff had known that. He could have been another Logan Carrington, could have used his power and influence many times to make life easier. But Jeff hadn't needed the trappings of money and position to make him the most wonderful man she had ever known. She didn't know how she could ever have remotely likened Logan Carrington to Jeff! 'I think you'd better leave,' she said distantly.

'Callie——'

'Please,' she shook her head. 'The same friend also said that money warps people, and after tonight I'm inclined to agree with that too.'

Logan drew in an angry breath, his nostrils flaring, his lips thinning. 'Maybe we were better off not knowing about each other.' He picked up his jacket. 'I wasn't aware that I was spending the evening with a narrow-minded girl who's easily influenced by other people's misguided opinions.'

'I'm not——'

'Aren't you?' He shrugged his shoulders into the velvet jacket. 'You've just quoted the opinions of some long-haired lout who's read his way through a few Marxist books and now thinks he's an authority on socialism. Tell me, Callie, if it works so well why are so many people defecting from Russia?'

'I——'

'Because it doesn't work, that's why,' he told her coldly. 'On paper it's Eden, all for one and one for all. But in theory it's just oppression at its worst. Okay, so I have money, and I made it by producing such *frivolous* things as cosmetics and perfumes. Maybe your young friend should take a vacation in one of these socialist countries, see how those people really live!'

She had opened a hornets' nest. Logan flushed with anger, his eyes cold. 'I didn't mean——'

'No, I'm sure you didn't,' he sneered. 'Go back to your socialist friends, Callie. And in future I'll stick to my rule not to get involved with impressionable children!'

'Logan——'

'Goodbye, Callie!'

He slammed the flat door so loud as he left that Paul instantly woke up, taking her attention for the next half an hour. But Logan was right about the talking. Paul slowly drifted back to sleep as she rocked him in the chair, murmuring softly to him all the time.

The flat seemed very quiet when she came out of the nursery, and strangely lonely too, the only reminder of Logan's presence here this evening the faint aroma of his aftershave.

She hadn't meant to anger him, and he had been completely wrong about Jeff. He hadn't been a socialist, he had felt that if someone worked for what they earnt then they were entitled to it, but he had obviously felt that the money he received from Spencer Plastics was not made by his merit but because of who he was. She hadn't meant to imply that Logan hadn't worked for his money, hadn't wanted him to storm out of here never to see him again.

And she wouldn't see him again, she knew that. Heavens, if only he knew, she was just as much of a capitalist as he was, was part owner of a successful firm, had so much money coming to her she didn't know what to do with it!

It got so late that in the end she dozed on the sofa, receiving one telephone call from Bill to tell her that there had been no change in his father-in-law's condition.

There had been no further word from him when she finally crawled, stiff with discomfort, from the sofa at seven o'clock the next morning. Paul would be waking for his breakfast in a minute, and what he was going to make of the absence of both his mother and father she had no idea. But she could take a good guess.

She had thought a lot about Logan Carrington during the long silent night, and she had decided she owed him an apology. Whether she had meant to or not, she had passed judgment on him, had been scornful and condescending about his way of life. She had been hypocritical, and she deserved his anger.

When Bill arrived home at seven-fifteen she was glad of his help with the inconsolable Paul. The poor baby was crying as if everyone had deserted him! And maybe to him it seemed as if they had.

But the arrival of his 'Dad-dee' did a lot to calm

him, so much so that Callie even managed to get some cereal down him while she listened to Bill.

'The doctor thinks Ted's going to pull through now, the worst is over, thank God. But Edith, Marilyn's mother, collapsed when the doctor told her he should be all right. Marilyn wants to move in with her mother for a while, and I think it's probably the best thing too.'

'Yes,' Callie nodded understandingly. 'Although I'll miss you.'

'Let's hope it won't be for too long,' Bill said ruefully. 'I know Ted's ill, and Edith needs us, but I'm not sure I can take living with her for too long.'

'I'm sure it won't be for long,' she assured him, being quite familiar with the discord between Bill and his in-laws. 'You have to come back for Christmas, it will be Paul's first real one. He was only three months old last year.'

'That's five weeks away. You don't think we'll be away that long?' he groaned.

'I hope not,' she grinned.

Bill frowned. 'You weren't frightened here on your own last night?'

Callie suddenly became very interested in feeding Paul his cereal. 'No, I was fine.' She didn't feel now was the time to tell Bill that she hadn't spent the evening alone, just the night.

'Was Paul good?'

'Oh yes.' She went on to tell him about the new trick of talking the baby to sleep.

'I'll tell Marilyn,' he said absently. 'Hey, would you mind packing Paul's things while I deal with Marilyn's and mine? Then you'll have to be getting to work, won't you?'

'Heavens, yes,' she groaned. 'I'd forgotten!'

'Well, from what I've discovered about Spencer Plastics so far you soon won't have to work another day of your life if you don't want to. I have to agree with your opinion of Sir Charles, he's a snob of the first degree. He refused to see me at first, until I told his secretary I was your lawyer, *then* he was falling over himself to be polite.' He smiled with remembered enjoyment. 'I put on my most haughty air.'

'Good for you!' she laughed, lifting Paul down from his high-chair and carrying him through to the bathroom for his wash.

Bill followed, to help in the washing of his son. 'I'm in the middle of doing a report for you. I'm afraid Ted's stroke will put that back for a while. I'm going to have trouble doing my ordinary job, let alone this extra work for you.'

'Don't worry about it,' she dismissed. 'The shareholders' meeting isn't for another three weeks, maybe you'll have it finished by then?'

'As there are only three of you, Sir Charles, his sister, and you, maybe they wouldn't mind cancelling it for a while? I don't want you going in there without all the facts.'

And she didn't want to go grovelling to Sir Charles for more time either! 'Maybe you could arrange that, if you get time,' she added hopefully.

'Of course,' he agreed instantly. 'It's the least I can do. Just don't worry about it for a while. And when you do go to the meeting I'll be with you.'

'Thanks, Bill,' she said gratefully. 'Now let's get this little man dressed and his suitcase packed. 'You're going to stay with Nanny, poppet,' she told him.

'But not for too long,' Bill muttered as he went into

his own bedroom to start packing.

Callie gave a husky laugh, although her smile faded as Bill drove off with Paul in the back of the car. It was going to be lonely in the flat knowing Bill and Marilyn weren't next door if she needed them.

She had to rush around to get ready for work, only just making it on time. Her job as personal secretary to the manager of an advertising agency was a hectic one at the best of times, giving her no time for her personal call to Logan.

'You look a little peaked,' her boss remarked as she went to lunch first. 'Late night?'

Callie was used to his probing into her personal life, his lightly flirtatious manner, and she fended it off with her usual flip comment, waiting until he had left the office before slumping down in her chair. Her lack of sleep from the night before was beginning to catch up with her now, and the thought of an early night was very inviting.

But now was no time to collapse with exhaustion; she had the perfect opportunity to call Logan Carrington. Luckily Carrington Cosmetics were in the phone book, although getting through to Logan wasn't so easy. He was right, his new secretary was very competent, so competent that she refused to put Callie through to his office, merely taking the message that she had called and her own telephone number.

So much for that, she thought with a frown. Oh well, if he was interested he would take her call as a sign that she was sorry for the way they had parted and would call her back.

There was no return call by the time she went to lunch, and the afternoon proved as fruitless. As the time passed she became more and more despondent.

She told herself it was because she didn't like to be bad friends with anyone, but she knew that wasn't the real reason. Logan Carrington had made a big impression on her, and it was him in particular she didn't want to be bad friends with.

Besides, her mother had always told her never to let the sun go down on an argument, and she had already let one night pass.

By four-thirty she had gained enough courage to call again, but the secretary put her off for a second time, saying Logan wasn't in the office, but that yes, she had given him the message before he left.

So that was that. Logan had received her message but hadn't followed it up. There was nothing more she could do.

It was just her luck that she had to work late that evening, her tiredness a physical as well as mental thing now, her movements sluggish and disjointed— not least because of Logan's lack of communication. She had liked him, really liked him, and she had thought he liked her. She must have been wrong. One little argument couldn't have changed his opinion so completely.

'Well, that's it.' Mike sat back with a sigh. 'You can type that report in the morning, Callie.'

'Right.' She didn't have the energy to do it now anyway!

He looked at his wrist-watch. 'I think I've made you late for your date.'

She gave a rueful smile, shaking her head. 'I don't have a date.'

'Of course you do.'

'No.'

'Oh hell!' he groaned, searching through the piles of

papers on his desk. 'I took this message for you while you were at lunch,' he handed her a slip of paper. 'I forgot to give it to you,' he added regretfully.

She read it with avid eyes, then looked up frowningly. 'It just says eight o'clock, Roberto's.'

'Well, that's what the man said,' Mike shrugged. 'He was in a hurry, said he wouldn't have the chance to call again. And could you meet him there.'

'Who is *he*, Mike?' she asked exasperatedly, wanting to be sure of her facts before she gave a whoop of joy.

'Well, I thought you'd know that,' he grumbled. 'I didn't bother to write his name down, and I've forgotten it now. I'm not used to taking down messages about dates for my secretary.'

Callie blushed. 'I'm sorry about that, Mike. But please try and remember the name.' There was always the possibility that she was wrong and that it wasn't Logan. She wouldn't start celebrating until she was sure.

Mike looked thoughtful. 'It began with an M, I think. Malcolm . . .? Morgan . . .? No, I remember now,' he smiled, 'his name was Logan. Ring any bells?'

'Oh yes!' she cried excitedly, standing up to hug him. 'Thank you, Mike. Oh, thank you!' Logan had called after all. He had called!

'He's special, hmm?'

'He could be,' she admitted shyly. 'If we ever get past the stage of arguing all the time.'

'Mm, he sounded the forceful type.'

'He is,' she nodded.

'And you aren't backwards in coming forward yourself,' Mike said ruefully. 'Callie, I hate to interrupt your ecstasy, but it's seven-thirty now, and if

I remember correctly, Roberto's is on the other side of town.'

'Lord, yes! And I have to go home and change. I'll never make it,' she groaned.

'Of course you will. Now just calm down,' Mike soothed. 'You drive home, carefully, and I'll call Roberto's and tell this Logan you're going to be a little late.'

'Would you really do that?' she gasped.

'Yes,' he laughed. 'After all, it's my fault you're late. Now off you go—and be careful.'

'Yes, sir,' she said cheekily before hurrying out of the office.

The traffic was heavy, and she seemed to have to stop at every set of traffic lights, drumming her fingertips impatiently on the steering wheel until the lights turned to green. Then the lift at the flats was out of order, meaning she had to run up the six flights to the flat, and then the telephone was ringing when she got in. It was Marilyn, and so Callie talked soothingly with her friend for ten minutes while she told her all about her father's illness, the problem of her own lateness for a date, even with Logan, completely unimportant by comparison.

She finally got off the telephone, found the shower water was cold, and then there was a stain on the dress she intended wearing. She didn't have that many evening dresses, so she was left with the brown velvet she had been wearing the night she and Logan had met. When she had finished getting ready she still wasn't satisfied with her appearance, but it was already eight-fifteen and Logan wouldn't wait for ever. He hadn't come across as a patient man at all.

Once again everything seemed to be out to delay

her—the traffic lights, a little old lady strolling across the road as if she had nothing better to do with her time. By the time Callie arrived at the restaurant she was in a complete state of panic, sure that Logan would have left by now, despite Mike's promise to call and let him know she would be late. It was almost nine o'clock, Logan certainly wasn't the type to sit around for an hour waiting for a woman, and certainly not one he had argued with the night before.

The doorman looked very formal and correct, and she hesitated about entering, conscious of the elegance and obvious wealth of the other people patronising this fashionable restaurant.

Logan was sure to have left by now, and——

'Can I help you?' The doorman had approached her.

'Er—I'm a little late, but I—I think Mr Carrington may be expecting me inside——'

'Mr Carrington?' His haughty manner instantly changed to one of deference. 'Mr Logan Carrington?'

It was amazing what the mention of a man with money could do to these people, she thought ruefully. 'Yes, that's right. You see——'

'And you would be Miss Day, Miss Callie Day?'

Her eyes widened. 'You know me?'

He gave her a look that said 'hardly'. 'Mr Carrington told us to expect you. We're to show you straight in.'

She wondered if he consciously used the royal 'we' or if it was done without him realising it!

'Then Mr Carrington hasn't left?' she said eagerly.

'Mr Carrington?' The man frowned. 'I was led to believe that the two of you were dining here.'

'Oh, we are. But—Oh, never mind,' she dismissed.

'Maybe I'd better just go inside.'

'Certainly, Miss Day.' He held the door open for her.

Thank goodness she was wearing her best dress; this place was for the élite with a capital E. There was a bar to the left of her, where several people were having a pre- or after-dinner drink, the women dripping diamonds, the men all in meticulously tailored suits, cigar smoke drifting to the ceiling. It was the sort of place Logan would feel at home in, but she wasn't so sure she——

Then she saw him, and the diamonds and obvious show of wealth didn't mean a thing. He had been sitting at the bar, but he was coming towards her now, the black dinner suit and snowy white shirt emphasising the darkness of his hair, the tan of his skin.

'Callie!' His hands came out to grasp hers, his gaze warm as he looked at her.

'Logan . . .' she breathed, spellbound, sure that she was falling in love with this man. She blushed with the confusion of her thoughts. 'I'm sorry I'm late. Mike said he would call——'

'He did,' Logan confirmed huskily.

'It was so disastrous. He forgot to give me your message, all the lights were against me, the lift was out of order, my dress had a stain, and then——'

'Hush,' Logan placed gentle fingertips over her lips. 'You're here now, that's all that matters.'

'Yes,' she agreed huskily, knowing that it was, that Logan was as aware of the spell of love being wound about them as she was.

CHAPTER FOUR

THEY gazed into each other's eyes for timeless minutes, and Logan was the one to finally break the spell. 'Are you ready to eat? Or would you like a drink first?' he asked briskly, probably as puzzled by what was happening to them as she was. 'I think I should warn you,' he added ruefully, 'I've already spent an hour in the bar.'

Callie laughed, as the mood lightened, the tension eased. 'Then I think we'd better eat. This is the last place you want to be thrown out of for being drunk and disorderly,' she teased, giving her jacket to the waiter.

Logan's hand on her arm was compelling. 'I'm not drunk, Callie—at least, not with wine. You understand?'

She swallowed hard, understanding perfectly. 'Yes,' she said huskily.

His arm was about her waist as he hugged her to his side. 'I really think you do. Let's go and eat,' he said more practically. 'We can talk over our meal.'

She didn't even care what she was to eat, leaving it to Logan to order the food for them both, gazing at him with adoring eyes as they talked.

'How is your friend's father?' he asked once the waiter had left with their order.

His thoughtfulness warmed her. He was a busy man, he must have had many other things on his mind all day, and yet he hadn't forgotten Marilyn's father.

71

'He's a lot better. Actually, that was another reason I was late. Marilyn called just as I got home, and——'

Logan laughed softly, his hand holding hers across the table. 'The odds really were against you, weren't they?'

'Yes,' she smiled too, her expression suddenly serious. 'I want to apologise for last night—yes,' she insisted as he shook his head.

'No,' he said firmly. 'Over the years I've received a lot of criticism from a lot of hotheads who don't seem to realise there have to be people like me, that this country needs industry. I think I overreacted to some of the things you said, took out my frustrated anger towards them on you. I'm the one who's sorry.'

'No——'

'Oh yes. I'm also sorry I couldn't pick you up this evening. A family crisis involved my driving out of town, and it was late when I got back.'

'Your mother . . .?'

'Is fine. It's the rest of them I could do without. Let's not discuss them,' he dismissed with impatience. 'I get angry just thinking about them.'

'And do you still get angry when you realise you're out with a twenty-two-year-old?'

'I asked for that,' he groaned. 'I wouldn't want you another day older than you are—but neither would I want you a day younger,' he added hastily.

Callie laughed. 'Poor Logan,' she teased.

'Lucky Logan,' he corrected. 'But I believe my secretary wouldn't put your call through today?' he added hardly.

'It was understandable. She didn't know who I was——'

'She does now,' he said grimly. 'And from now on

your calls will be put straight through to me.'

She eyed him mockingly. 'What makes you think I'm going to call you again?'

'You'd better!' he said with mock sternness. 'I'm going to insist you call me every day from now on.'

Her heart gave a happy leap. 'My boss won't like that,' she teased gently.

'In that case I'll call you,' he said determinedly.

'And what would we find to talk about every day?'

'The evenings we're going to spend together.'

'Logan!' she laughed. 'You can't telephone me every day and then want to see me every evening too.'

'Who says I can't?' he was arrogant.

'Well, I——'

'I'm not losing you, Callie.' He was deadly serious now. 'I knew there was something different about you the moment I met you. I'd like to explore that special something about you over the next few weeks.'

'I'd like that too,' she admitted huskily.

The rest of the evening passed in a daze for Callie. She and Logan discussed everything under the sun, discovered similar tastes in books and music, a liking for ballet.

'I usually take my mother if she's in town,' Logan told her on the drive back to her flat. 'Maybe I could take you both some time. The Festival Ballet are going to be in town next month,' he added thoughtfully.

She gave a start of surprise at his mention of her meeting his mother. In her eyes meeting a man's parents, especially a man of Logan's age, meant he was serious about her. Oh, she hoped so!

This evening with Logan had been the most enjoyable she had spent in a long time, and she hoped they would have many more of them together. Logan's possessive manner seemed to say they would.

'. . . would that be all right with you?' he was asking now.

'Er—— Sorry?' She had been so deep in thought she hadn't heard a word he said!

'Sleepyhead,' he chided softly, his smile warm. 'I said my mother usually likes to see *Swan Lake*, it's her favourite. How about if I arrange tickets for the three of us?'

'When would it be for?'

'A few weeks' time. Does it matter?' he frowned.

'I was just wondering if I would still be seeing you then.' She eyed him mockingly. 'I read an article about you in a magazine once, it said your girl-friends last an average of four weeks.'

His mouth twisted. 'In my maturity that's increased to two months,' he derided.

'In that case, get the tickets. I should just make it!'

'I can't wait to reach your flat,' he muttered.

Her eyes widened. 'Wanting to get rid of me already?'

'No,' he said grimly.

'Then what—— Oh,' she blushed as his gaze caressed her, 'I see.'

'Do you?' he chuckled.

'You like teasing me!'

'And you like teasing me.'

'Yes . . .'

'Well, fair's fair. And I like your teasing, Callie. Although this time you're wrong.'

'Wrong?' she frowned.

His hand came out to grasp hers. 'You'll be in my life a lot longer than two months.'

'Will I?' she said breathlessly.

'You know you will.'

'Maybe I need—convincing.'

'Maybe I intend—convincing,' Logan said throatily. 'Maybe that's the reason I can't wait to get to your home.'

Callie was flushed with excitement by the time Logan parked the car outside her home, although she let out a groan as she saw the 'Out of Order' sign still on the lift. 'I should have realised, British workmen being what they are, that the lift won't be mended until tomorrow.'

'Lazybones,' he mocked. 'Think of the poor people who live above you.'

'Goodness, yes. There are fifteen floors altogether,' she realised as they trudged up the stairs.

To give Logan his due he wasn't even breathing heavily by the time they had walked up the six flights, whereas she was puffing away like an old woman.

'You're out of condition,' he taunted as he took her key from her hand, opening the door to switch on the light. 'Mm, nice,' he commented, appreciative of the uncluttered homeliness of her home.

'Thanks,' she moved to switch on the electric fire. 'And I'm not out of condition, I happen to have walked up and down those stairs already once tonight.'

'So you do,' he smiled. 'Come and rest, Callie,' he pulled her down on the sofa beside him.

'Maybe I can get you some coffee? Or a drink? Or——'

'You?' he asked throatily.

She swallowed hard. 'No, not me. I told you, I always sleep alone.'

'And I heard you.' His voice hardened. 'And I

respect that. Going to bed with you wasn't what I had in mind.' He had moved away from her, both physically and mentally.

She put her hand out to him as he stood up. 'Logan, I'm sorry——'

'I know I have a reputation.' He was prowling the room. 'But I hadn't met you then. Do you know that I didn't even sleep last night after I walked out of here?' he rasped.

'Neither did I,' she admitted softly.

'And that I've thought of nothing but you since Saturday night?'

'Neither have I.'

'I've known you only four days, Callie.' He pulled her up into his arms. 'And yet I feel differently with you than with any other woman.'

'Yes.'

'You can feel it too?'

'Yes.'

He frowned, shaking his head. 'I can't understand it.'

Callie gently touched his rigid jaw, understanding that part of the reason for his mercurial moods was his complete puzzlement with the way he felt about her. 'Do you have to?'

'A week ago, *five days ago*, I hadn't even met you, now I don't like to think how empty my life was without you.'

'It wasn't empty, Logan,' she shook her head. 'You had other interests, other friends——'

'Other friends, yes,' he acknowledged bitterly. 'Sexual friends. Does that bother you?'

'Does it bother you?'

'At the time, no. Now——'

'You can never go back and change your life, Logan,' she interrupted softly. 'If you were happy with it at the time then now you just have to accept it.'

He looked down at her frowningly. 'Another quote from this male friend of yours?'

'It didn't sound like me, hmm?' she said ruefully.

'It sounded like someone who's lived life a lot longer than you have.'

'You're right,' she smiled. 'He was a lot older than me, but the wisest, gentlest——'

'Careful,' Logan warned gruffly, 'or I'll be getting jealous!'

'You have no need to be. He's dead now, so he can't hurt you,' she said dully.

'I'm sorry,' his regret was genuine.

'So am I,' she bit her lip. 'I'll tell you about him some time—but not yet.'

'The wound's still too raw, is it?'

She wouldn't have exactly called it a wound, more a deep loss. But he was right, it was too recent for her to talk about Jeff unemotionally.

'Kiss me, Logan,' she invited huskily.

'Oh, I intend to,' he drawled. 'Very thoroughly. In fact, I've been looking forward to it.'

'You have?'

'Haven't you?'

He must know she had. All through dinner, the drive here, they had been aware only of each other, the sensual tension building up by the second.

As their lips met Callie felt as if she had come home, as if she had found the other half of herself, their bodies fitting perfectly together.

'Oh, Callie, Callie,' Logan murmured between kisses, gently probing the edge of her lips, his hands at her nape releasing the single fastening of the halter-necked dress, the soft velvet material like a caress as it fell down to her waist, her breasts bared to his questing hands, touching her nipples until she arched against him.

'Logan!' she gasped as his hand closed firmly over one taut pink nub, bending her back over his arm as he thoroughly explored each rosy peak with leisurely ease, his hands moving up and down her spine in a slow caress.

'Callie, this may be insane,' he groaned against her flesh, 'but I think I'm falling in love with you!'

'Only think?'

'After thirty-five years I'm not sure I'd recognise it if it hit me in the face,' he admitted ruefully. 'But I do know I'm more attracted to you than to any other woman I've ever met. I also know I think about you all the time I'm away from you.'

'That's enough for now,' she smoothed the hair at his temples, lovingly noticing a sprinkling of grey among its dark thickness.

Logan raised his head to look at her. 'Is it?' he frowned.

'Yes,' she kissed the side of his mouth. 'We have time, Logan, plenty of time.'

'Yes . . .' His mouth once more claimed hers.

Callie responded without reserve, more sure than Logan, knowing that this was the man she loved, the man she wanted to be with for all time.

She slipped his jacket from his shoulders, unbuttoning his shirt, until their heated flesh seared together, her nipples hardened against his rougher skin. It was all happening so beautifully, so naturally, that there was no thought of denial, only rising pleasure, a deep ache in the pit of her stomach that was almost a pain.

And Logan was as affected as she was, a glazed look to his eyes as he kissed her throat and breasts, his breathing ragged, the pulsating of his thighs heavy against hers.

'No more.' He put her away from him with a groan.

'Logan . . .?' she reached out for him.

'No, Callie!' He closed his eyes to her as he fought for control. 'For once in my life I'm going to do this right. I'm no saint, darling,' he buttoned his shirt, smoothing back his tousled hair. 'Far from it, in fact,' he added derisively. 'But I'm not going to rush anything with you. Like you said, we have time.'

She felt disappointment, sitting up to refasten the halter-neck at her nape, her hair becoming entangled in the button.

'Here, let me,' Logan offered, his fingers impersonal against her nape.

Callie trembled with reaction; she was not sophisticated enough to deal with the sexual disappointment as easily as Logan seemed to. He turned her gently to face him, his eyes darkening to a smoky grey as he saw the tears shimmering in her eyes.

'Darling, don't cry,' he pulled her into his arms with a groan. 'Don't cry, Callie,' he smoothed her hair in soothing movements.

'I'm sorry,' she sniffed. 'I-It——'

'I know, my darling,' he said softly. 'And I'm sorry. But I don't want to ruin anything between us.' His hands cradled each side of her face. 'Forgive me?'

Forgive him for not making love to her? She should be thanking him! She had been beyond saying no herself, had been lost in mindless wonder of her love for this man. And yet she didn't feel like thanking him, still ached for him.

'Callie?'

She drew a shaky breath. 'There's nothing to forgive,' she gave a jerky smile. 'I should be relieved you said no——'

'I didn't say no,' he groaned, his eyes still dark. 'I just said not yet.'

'Yes,' she smoothed the skirt of her dress. 'Would you like some coffee now?'

'No, thanks.' He pulled on his jacket, doing up the buttons to his shirt. 'I have to go. Lunch tomorrow?'

'I——'

'It will save the telephone call,' he encouraged.

'But not my waistline!' Callie joined in his lighter mood, glad that Logan was controlling the situation, knowing that he was right to do so.

'Your waistline doesn't need saving,' he said huskily. 'It's perfect as it is.'

'That's what I mean,' she teased. 'I don't want to get any fatter.'

'You aren't fat, you're perfect.' He held her hands in his. 'Please meet me for lunch, Callie. It's such a long time until the evening.'

She felt the same way, and despite the fact that Logan had admitted to being anything but an innocent where women were concerned, she knew this wasn't a line—and that he was as bewildered by this overwhelming attraction as she was.

'All right, lunch. But we can't go out to dinner too, or I really will get fat. Come here for the evening,' she suggested eagerly.

A pulse beat erratically at his jawline. 'I don't think that would be a good idea.'

'Oh, Logan——'

'We have to meet on mutual ground, Callie,' he insisted. 'It's the only way I can get through this. We'll go to a club I know, have a few drinks, dance a little.'

'Dance?' she said hopefully.

'Yes,' he gave a rueful smile. 'I think I can trust myself that much.'

'I hope not,' she taunted.

'Callie,' he laughed softly, 'you aren't very good for my self-control!'

'And you aren't very good for mine,' she said throatily.

'Lunch,' he said briskly. 'I know the agency you work for, so I'll pick you up.'

He called for her every day that week, and the next, meeting her every evening too. For Callie the attraction was still as fresh and strong, and as she watched the way Logan merited respect wherever they went, for a meal, to the theatre, a club, her love deepened. He continued to treat her with easy charm that came so naturally to him, the intensity of their second evening spent together kept firmly at bay.

In the middle of the second week Bill telephoned her to say he had managed to get the shareholders' meeting put off until the New Year. 'Although Sir Charles wasn't very pleased about it,' he added with satisfaction.

'Poor Sir Charles,' she said unsympathetically.

'That's what I thought.' The grin could be heard in his voice. 'Not least of his gripes seemed to be that you aren't seeing his son any more.'

'Thank God!' she groaned.

'I gathered from Marilyn that he wasn't exactly the

catch of the season. But Sir Charles doesn't seem very happy about you spoiling all his plans.'

'Plans for me to marry his son,' she said disgustedly. 'I never heard of anything so archaic!'

'No. By the way, I've been calling you the past three nights and getting no reply. Found yourself a boyfriend?' he teased much as an older brother might.

'As a matter of fact, yes,' she admitted shyly.

'Good for you!' Bill sounded genuinely pleased. 'Marilyn and I have been worried about you since Jeff died,' he added softly.

'I know,' she said huskily. 'And I appreciate it. But I've met someone, Bill, and—well, he—he's just wonderful.'

'I can tell,' he chuckled. 'Wait until I tell Marilyn!'

Callie knew her friend would be overjoyed, that Bill was too. They really had been very good to her since Jeff died. 'Once you're back home I'll have you all over for dinner,' she promised.

'Must be serious if you're actually going to cook,' Bill teased.

Callie laughed too. Almost everyone who knew her also knew that she hated to cook, even more so since she had been on her own. 'This will be a special occasion,' she explained.

'It must be!'

'Bill . . .!' she warned.

'Okay, okay,' he laughed. 'Ted's well on the way to recovery now, although it's a slow process. But we'll be home soon, Marilyn can't stand being in the kitchen with her mother,' he said with satisfaction. 'And Paul is really getting spoilt.'

'Sounds like you're having fun,' Callie commented.

'Oh, we are!'

'At least I'm glad about Marilyn's father.'

'We all are,' he said seriously. 'I'll speak to you again next week. You never know, I should have that report ready as a Christmas present.'

'Thanks,' she laughed.

'Seriously, Callie, would you like someone else to do it?'

'Seriously, Bill, no. Christmas is only three weeks away, and as the meeting isn't until New Year I don't need it yet. About Christmas——'

'I doubt we'll be back, Callie,' he said regretfully. 'Maybe your boy-friend will keep you company.'

She hadn't dared to think as far away as Christmas, although the thought of spending the time with Logan filled her with warm anticipation. Just thinking about Logan at all filled her with warmth. 'Maybe,' she agreed non-committally. 'But I'll still miss little Paul.'

'I see,' Bill mocked.

She was instantly contrite. 'I didn't mean it like that!'

'I know you didn't,' he laughed. 'Look, I have to go now, love, but Marilyn will probably call you for a chat in the week—if you can be reached!'

'I don't usually go out until eight o'clock, and I'm home by six. That gives you two hours to——'

'I'm only joking, Callie,' he teased. 'Only joking. But tell him he's a lucky man.'

'But I already knew it,' Logan said later that evening when she passed on Bill's message.

'Flatterer,' she blushed.

'Not at all. And I would like us to spend Christmas together,' he added deeply.

Happiness lit her face, only to fade seconds later. 'But won't you be spending it with your mother?'

'If she's back by then,' he said dryly, 'we can both spend it with her.'

'Back?' Callie sipped her wine.

He nodded, very dark and distinguished in his black evening suit. 'I had a call from her this afternoon, she told me she had to get away from the family pressure.'

Callie's brows rose. 'You?'

'No,' his mouth quirked with amusement, 'not me. My mother is in business with my uncle, and just lately he's been more pushy than usual. I don't have a lot of time for my uncle's machinations myself. Anyway, the outcome of it is that my mother has gone to Switzerland to stay with a couple of her cronies. She could be back before Christmas, but then again she may not be.'

'Then that means the ballet is off.' Callie hid her disappointment well. Meeting Logan's mother had been like a talisman to her. The passion they had shared on their second evening together had never been repeated, in fact Logan hadn't been in her flat since, and the thought of meeting his mother had given her hope that he might feel as seriously about their relationship as she did. Now that stability had been taken away from her.

'No, I'll still take you.' He clasped her hand as it lay on the table. 'After all, I already have the tickets.'

She didn't care about seeing the ballet, it was not seeing his mother that upset her. 'That will be nice,' she sighed.

He frowned. 'You don't sound very enthusiastic.'

She gave a bright, meaningless smile. 'Sorry.'

'If you don't want to go——'

'Of course I want to go,' she contradicted, shaking off her feelings of disappointment with effort. After all, Logan had invited her to spend Christmas with himself and his mother. That was even better than the ballet.

But Mrs Carrington seemed in no hurry to come back to England, and two days before Christmas Logan had still had no word of her return.

'It's nothing unusual,' he dismissed her show of concern. 'She often has these impromptu holidays, to get away from my uncle. But there's no reason why we shouldn't spend Christmas together.'

'Your place or mine?' Callie said cryptically. So far she hadn't seen Logan's apartment, as Logan had kept to his decision that they meet on mutual ground. But they could hardly spend Christmas in a restaurant, not even one as elegant as the one they were eating in tonight!

His mouth quirked with amusement. 'That's a point,' he said dryly. 'Maybe my mother will get back after all.'

'Logan——'

'Logan, *darling*!' purred a seductively female voice. 'How lovely to see you again! You've been quite unsociable lately, darling,' she added reprovingly, bending towards him over the table.

Callie looked up at the most beautiful woman she had ever seen, the thickly waving red hair was strangely familiar to her. Of course, the night she and Logan had met! This was the beautiful Danielle, the woman Logan had stopped seing in preference to her.

The woman stood almost six feet in height, her model-girl figure barely covered by the low-cut backless dress, although the dress was worn with such grace and style that it couldn't possibly be offensive. As Callie looked into her face she was amazed at the hardness of the blue eyes, although the hardness disappeared as her gaze returned to Logan.

He had stood up as soon as Danielle spoke, the two of them of similar height. 'Danielle,' he greeted tightly.

'Aren't you going to introduce us, darling?' She looked pointedly at Callie, the expensive perfume she wore slightly overpowering, certainly not the lighter Passion that she modelled for Logan's company.

He made the introductions stiltedly, obviously not welcoming this interruption by his ex-girl-friend. Callie had an idea that when an affair ended for Logan then it ended for good. She shivered at the thought of their own relationship ending the same way.

'Are you here alone?' He spoke politely enough to the other woman, although there was a steel edge to his voice.

'Hardly,' she scorned such a question. 'David is just collecting my wrap. The mink you bought me, actually, darling,' she drawled.

'Really?' His tone cooled even more.

Callie was beginning to pity Danielle now, beautiful as the other woman was. She was pushing Logan to the limit of his politeness, and considering the role the other woman had once had in his life she would have thought she would have known that. But perhaps Danielle was past caring? It certainly seemed that way!

'Yes,' Danielle continued, 'you always did have wonderful taste.'

'Most of the time,' he muttered grimly.

Blue eyes flashed. 'And what does Callie do?' She made the question sound like an insult. 'Is she your latest—model?'

A pulse worked angrily at Logan's jaw, although he

remained otherwise calm. 'Callie is a secretary,' he revealed tightly.

'Really?' Arched eyebrows rose. 'That makes a change. Although I do remember Jenny was leaving you. Strange, I never thought you the type of man to chase his secretary around the office all day.'

'Callie isn't my secretary, Danielle,' he said tautly.

'What a shame—for you. Have you bought her a fur yet?' she added spitefully.

'Danielle——'

'And the diamonds. Don't forget the diamonds. You have the most wonderful taste in jewellery too, Logan.'

'Danielle——'

'Am I talking too much, darling?' Her voice was brittle. 'I thought it was the man who wasn't supposed to kiss and tell?'

Logan was rigid with anger. 'And I believed it was a two-way thing,' he rasped.

'I just thought your little friend, your young friend—God, you are young, aren't you?' Danielle frowned down at Callie. 'Oh well,' she shrugged, 'I suppose you know what you're doing.' Her gaze returned to Logan. 'I just thought Callie should know the routine with you, the way you like the pursuit, to rush a girl off her feet—and into your bed, then drop her when the next beauty takes your fancy. That is your way, isn't it, Logan?' she scorned.

'I think you've said enough——'

'Quite enough,' she agreed brightly. 'I do hope you enjoy your meal.' She walked away with an exaggerated sway of her slender hips.

Logan was furious, and Callie knew she was supposed to be upset, and yet somehow she wasn't.

Her feelings were ones of sympathy, for Danielle, that she still cared enough for Logan to hit out in that bitchy way, a way guaranteed to alienate him even though it must have given her tremendous satisfaction at the time.

Logan was still standing, had stood all during the conversation with Danielle, his eyes glittering dangerously now, his mouth a grim line. 'Let's get out of here,' he rasped, taking Callie's hand in his and pulling her to her feet.

She frowned her consternation. 'We haven't even eaten yet!'

He sighed his impatience. 'You're hungry?'

'Well, I—— Yes.' It might be mundane, but it was the truth. She had been too busy at work today to bother about lunch, and her stomach was now protesting loudly at the omission.

'We'll eat at my apartment,' he told her derisively. 'I'm sure my housekeeper can provide us with something.'

'But, Logan——'

'I know I said we should stay away from potentially dangerous situations,' he ran an agitated hand through the thickness of his hair, 'but I want to talk to you, and I certainly can't do it here. Will you come with me?'

She offered no more resistance, welcoming the chance to go to Logan's home. The restraint he had put on their relationship had meant they had shared no more than a brief if passionate goodnight kiss at the end of the evening, and the strain of it all was beginning to tell on her. They had been seeing each other for weeks now, and Logan controlled their meetings with the experience he had no trouble exerting. She welcomed this chance to be alone with him.

He had a beautiful home, with an elegance and style that Logan himself possessed. The lounge he took her into was on two levels, the sitting area almost seemed to be sunk into the floor, in several shades of brown and gold—like autumn, Callie thought wonderingly, the dining area being up three steps on the higher level.

Logan had just invited her to sit down when a middle-aged woman came into the room. Logan ordered her out again after asking her to prepare dinner for two. All the time he was talking to the housekeeper his gaze never left Callie.

To the other woman's credit she didn't even blink at suddenly being asked to produce a meal for two people, and Logan didn't seem to feel any awkwardness in asking her. Callie wondered what he would have made of the scratch meal she would have provided at such short notice—packet chips and eggs any style! The capable Mrs Brown looked as if she would provide something much more appetising than that.

Logan paced the room once they were alone, the anger that had possessed him all the way here now turning to charged tension. 'God, I could strangle her!' he muttered.

'Logan, please——'

'Danielle behaved disgracefully!'

'It doesn't matter,' she told him gently. 'Really it doesn't. You and she were close——'

'Too damned close!'

'The sort of closeness I would like,' she insisted softly, meeting his narrow-eyed gaze unflinchingly. 'The sort of closeness I want, Logan?'

'No!'

She paled. 'You don't want to make love to me?'

He came to sit down beside her. 'Not make love to you?' he groaned. 'I think I'll die if I can't soon see your face beside me when I wake up in the morning, carry the memory of your warm loving with me all day until I can get home and we make love all over again.'

Her pulse raced, warmth entering her cheeks. 'That's what I want too,' she told him huskily.

'Not quite,' he derided.

'But I do!'

'I haven't finished saying all that needs to be said.' He grimaced. 'What I'm trying to say, and not making a very good job of it, is that I don't just want an affair with you. I want more, much more. I want you beside me for the rest of my life, Callie.'

'Logan . . .?'

He drew in a deep breath. 'I want marriage, Callie.'

CHAPTER FIVE

'DARLING?' he prompted anxiously at her numbed silence, her wide-eyed disbelief.

Callie swallowed hard. 'But you don't get married! You never——'

'To *you* I get married.' He held both her hands in his, caressing life back into their chilled numbness. 'Callie, I love you. I want to marry you.'

He was so earnest, so sincere, that she could no longer doubt he meant every word he was saying. 'We hardly know each other——'

'I knew I loved you the moment I looked at you,' he insisted firmly. 'You were intelligent as well as beautiful. It's taken me some time to admit to the way I feel, but after tonight——! I don't intend leaving you open to any more barbs like the ones Danielle made tonight. You're special, not a part of some damned *routine* to get you into bed. Do you believe me, darling?'

She had never doubted that she meant more to him than any of the other women he had had in his life, had known by his physical restraint that he respected her—but marriage! It had never occurred to her, not even in her wildest daydreams about this man.

'Callie?'

She looked up at his pale, strained face, seeing the tension that surrounded him as he waited for her answer. 'Logan, I——'

'For God's sake don't turn me down!' he groaned.

'You have no idea how much I need you.'

She gave a breathless laugh. 'Only a fool would turn you down, Logan,' she smiled. 'And I hope I'm no fool.'

He drew in a ragged breath. 'Does that mean the answer is yes?'

Her amusement deepened, her eyes glowing with happiness. 'Don't look so surprised! I love you too, you see.'

'You do?'

'Of course.' She gave a choked laugh at his astonishment.

'Oh, Callie!' He enfolded her in his arms, his face buried against her throat. 'I thought you'd say no,' he rained kisses over her face and throat. 'I didn't think you would want me.'

She touched his face with trembling fingertips. 'I'm yours, Logan. I thought you already knew that.'

'I do now. Callie——'

'Dinner is ready, Mr—— oh!' a red-faced Mrs Brown stood in the now open doorway. 'I'm sorry, sir,' she said stiffly. 'I had no idea you were—occupied.' Her arms were folded disapprovingly across her ample bosom.

It took tremendous effort of will for Logan to answer the woman and keep a straight face. 'We'll be there in ten minutes, Mrs Brown,' he said dismissively.

'Yes, sir.' With another scathing look she left the room.

'Oh, Logan!' Callie giggled, snuggling into his arms. 'The poor woman was scandalised!'

'Damn Mrs Brown,' he growled. 'I'm the one you

should feel sorry for, I only have ten minutes to show you how much I love you!'

Her mouth quirked provocatively. 'Then you hadn't better waste any of it, had you?' she tempted.

Logan grinned. 'I think I'm going to like being married to you.'

'I hope so, because I don't intend sharing you,' she told him seriously.

'I doubt I'll have the time,' he murmured into her hair.

'I'll make sure of it.'

'Not like this you won't,' he taunted.

She stood on tiptoe to kiss him, gasping as Logan took over the initiative, his mouth at once demanding and possessive.

By the time they walked into the dining-room fifteen minutes later Callie knew herself to be thoroughly kissed—and by the disapproving look on Mrs Brown's face she knew it too!

'Perhaps you should tell her we're getting married,' Callie giggled. 'Then she might stop looking at me as though I'm one of your women.'

Logan gave what she thought of as 'one of his arrogant looks'. 'Even if you were just one of my "women",' he said haughtily, 'she has no right to look at you in any way. I shall talk to her——'

'Oh no, darling!' She clasped his hand as Mrs Brown served their dessert to them, a delicious orange concoction made with meringue. 'Please don't say anything to Mrs Brown, Logan,' she pleaded once they were alone. 'After all, I have to live here after we're married. I don't want to start off on the wrong foot with your housekeeper.'

'We don't have to keep her——'

'Logan, don't be so cold-hearted!' she complained.

'Mrs Brown is quite understandably a little surprised at your behaviour.'

'Oh?'

'Yes.' She held back a smile. 'I'm much too young for you,' she said mischievously.

'You——!'

'Yes?' She raised innocent eyebrows.

'Nothing—for now. I'll deal with you later,' he warned softly 'And I have no intention of telling Mrs Brown you've agreed to become my wife. My mother will be the first to know—if she ever gets back from Switzerland,' he frowned.

Her eyes glowed with happiness. 'Oh, Logan, it's going to be such fun being married to you!' She gave a lighthearted laugh of sheer pleasure.

'Fun?' he questioned the description.

'Oh yes,' she smiled. 'I love it when you forget to be all staid and respectable, forget you're thirty-five——'

'And you're twenty-two,' he groaned. 'I must be mad!'

'But you're going to continue being mad?' she asked anxiously.

'I don't think I can prevent it.'

'I do hope not.'

It was very late when Logan suggested driving her home, the two of them having talked into the early hours of the morning. One thing had been made passionately clear to Callie—Logan wanted her for his wife soon, he had no intention of waiting longer than the New Year.

'Would you like to come in?' she offered when they reached her home.

'I'd better not,' he shook his head. 'I'm too vulnerable.'

'*You* are?'

'I am,' he nodded. 'Now run along indoors before I change my mind.'

'I wish you would,' she pouted her disappointment.

'I intend introducing you to my mother without guilt,' he told her sternly. 'She isn't stupid, she knows the life I've led. I want her to know that with you it's been different from the start.'

Callie couldn't help but feel warmed by his desire to protect her, and she returned his goodnight kiss with a fervour that left them both gasping.

'Tomorrow night?' Logan murmured against her lips.

'Oh yes,' she agreed without hesitation.

'Christmas Eve,' he mused. 'I wonder what Father Christmas is going to bring you?'

'You?'

'Oh, you've already got me,' he chuckled. 'I've been trussed up and ready for the kill from the beginning.'

'Well, you're all I want, so Father Christmas can give me a miss this year.'

She had never felt so happy, so very much alive, and even the last-minute Christmas shoppers couldn't put her in a bad mood the next day as they pushed and shoved her about.

She had done her own shopping weeks before, had bought Logan an expensive aftershave set, but a prospective husband warranted something a little more personal. She found a beautiful pair of cufflinks, paying double for the engraving of Logan's initials, knowing that with the Christmas rush the man didn't really have the time to do them. They looked beautiful in their brown velvet box, and she only hoped Logan would like them.

'You're looking very pleased with yourself,' Mike remarked when she got back from her successful lunch-hour.

She wished she could tell him the real reason for her ecstatic happiness, but she understood and respected Logan's wish that his mother be the first to be told their news. She would have plenty of time after Christmas to tell all her own friends the happy news.

'It's Christmas,' she excused.

He grimaced. 'I suppose that means you want to go home early.'

The idea hadn't even occurred to her. Although it would be nice, there were still a few little presents she would like to get Logan, stocking-fillers. 'I hadn't thought about it . . .' She looked at Mike hopefully.

'But now that I've mentioned it . . .' he said dryly.

'Well . .'

'Okay,' he laughed. 'Tidy your desk and you can go. Oh, and call your boy-friend before you leave. It sounded urgent.'

Her eyes widened. 'Logan called?'

'About half an hour ago,' he nodded. 'See, I didn't forget this time.'

'Thanks, Mike,' she grinned, and went to her own desk to put the call through to Logan. Audrey Harris put her straight through to his office. She had met the other girl a couple of times when she had met Logan at his office if he was working late, and from the way she spoke about Logan it was obvious the infatuation was continuing. Callie had teased Logan about it only last night, claiming that perhaps it would stop when he was a married man. Logan had scowled, saying the stupid girl would probably just find him more intriguing. Stupid was the last thing Callie would have called Audrey Harris; the black-haired blue-eyed beauty was very intelligent, and made no secret of her envy of Callie.

'Hello, darling,' Logan interrupted her wandering thoughts. 'Good news—my mother gets back this evening.'

'That's wonderful!' And indeed it was, it meant she wouldn't have to keep her engagement to Logan a secret much longer.

She spared a thought for the poor Spencer family. What a shock they were going to get when they knew she was to marry Logan, that if Donald hadn't taken her to that party she would never have met him. How furious they would be if they knew Donald was responsible for losing the chance to get their hands on her shares. Poor Donald would probably have to leave the country!

'I wanted to meet you for lunch,' Logan continued. 'But your employer said you'd already left.'

'Last-minute Christmas shopping,' she smiled to herself, sure that he was going to like the cufflinks.

'My mother wants you to join us for the Christmas holiday.'

'You told her about me?' Callie gasped.

'No,' he chuckled. 'Much to her chagrin. She's bursting with curiosity, and all I would tell her was that I wanted her to meet a friend of mine.'

'Oh, Logan,' she chided, 'your poor mother!'

'She'll be overjoyed when I tell her the friend is to be my wife,' he said with satisfaction. 'Telling her over the telephone isn't what I had in mind at all. I have to go and meet her at the airport. Do you want to come along?'

'What time?'

'Seven-thirty.'

'I can't,' she refused regretfully. 'Bill is calling round this evening, and he said it would be between seven and eight.'

'I see,' he seemed to think for a moment. 'Well, never mind,' he dismissed. 'It's better if you meet her tomorrow anyway. She'll probably be tired after her flight.'

'I'll see you tomorrow, then?'

'You'll see me tonight,' he told her firmly. 'After I've dropped my mother off I'll be back in London to see you.'

'You don't have to——'

'Don't I?' he interrupted quietly.

'No.'

'And if I want to?' he drawled.

'Oh, that's different,' she said eagerly. 'If you aren't too late you can help me decorate the tree.'

'You haven't done that yet?' Logan sounded surprised.

'It's traditional in our family to decorate the tree on Christmas Eve.'

'I see. And is it going to be traditional in our family too?' He chuckled at her sudden silence. 'Callie, are you blushing?'

She was, deeply so. The prospect of having Logan as a husband was still so new to her that the idea of a family, of Logan's children, had come as something of a shock to her.

'Callie?' he laughed.

'I think you do it on purpose,' she said irritably.

'Do what?' he teased.

'I'm not going to humour you,' she told him haughtily. 'I'll see you later tonight.'

'It's traditional in *my* family to give presents on Christmas Eve. Would you like your present tonight?'

'That depends what it is,' she said guardedly.

'You're learning, Callie,' he chuckled. 'You're learning. But I guarantee you'll like this. I love you,' his voice lowered seductively.

'Me too,' she returned softly.

'Can't talk, hmm?' he guessed.

'No.' She was very conscious of Mike sitting at his desk a few feet away from her, this being one of the open-plan style offices that are so popular nowadays— and which offered no privacy for its occupants.

'But I can,' said Logan with obvious enjoyment. 'Tonight, when we're alone, I'm going to——'

'Behave yourself,' Callie warned.

'Or I'll make you blush again?' he mocked.

'Logan——'

'Okay, okay, I'm being unfair. But I will be back tonight, although it could be late. And tomorrow we'll drive to my mother's together.'

Callie quickly tidied her desk after ringing off, and hurried to the shops to buy a present for her future mother-in-law, choosing a beautiful cut-glass vase and buying some roses to put in it.

Bill arrived at twenty past seven. 'For you,' he handed her a gaily wrapped parcel.

'For you,' she laughingly handed him the presents she had bought for him, Marilyn, and Paul.

'I think we came out best in that exchange,' he grinned.

'You haven't seen what I bought you yet!' She thought gleefully of the lurid underpants she had bought him.

'I can imagine,' he grimaced, sitting down to undo

his briefcase. 'That report on Spencer Plastics I've been promising you——' He handed it to her, a brown folder that looked as if it would take some reading.

'Thanks.' She put it on the table.

'Hey!' Bill chided in a wounded voice. 'Aren't you even going to look at it?'

'It's Christmas, Bill——'

'And the whole world grinds to a halt,' he moaned.

'Just for one day,' she smiled.

'One?' he said disgustedly. 'It seems to get longer every year. Most places make no distinction between Christmas and New Year now.'

'Grouch!' she teased.

'Four days non-stop of Marilyn's mother and you'd be a grouch too,' he grimaced.

'Never mind, it will soon be over.'

'You're mighty cheerful for someone who's supposedly spending Christmas on her own.' He looked at her with questioning eyes.

Callie told him what he wanted to hear, that far from being alone she was going to be with Logan. 'Would you like a Christmas drink?' she offered.

'Whisky?' he asked hopefully.

'With water or without?'

'With, please. I guess he likes whisky,' Bill said thoughtfully.

'Hmm?' Callie asked vaguely as she prepared his drink.

'The new man in your life,' he sipped his whisky appreciatively, 'he drinks whisky, right?'

'Right.' She sat down opposite him, sipping her own Martini. 'But he's never been here—well, not after the first time anyway,' she blushed. 'I just got the whisky in because—well, because——'

'In case he did come in again,' Bill mocked.

'Yes.' Her blush deepened.

'And do you think he's going to?'

'Probably later tonight,' she revealed shyly, knowing that until Logan had told his mother their plans that she couldn't even tell her best friends she was going to marry him.

'Lucky you. I take it it's the same man?'

'Yes.'

'Marilyn will be pleased.'

'Marilyn already knows,' she taunted. 'I told her yesterday on the telephone.'

'She could have told me,' he moaned. 'So I suppose my report gets put aside until after the holiday?'

'Oh, at least until then,' she confirmed, thinking of her wedding in the New Year.

'So much for slaving long into the night——'

'Oh, Bill, you didn't!' She frowned her dismay, glaring at him as he grinned at her. 'No, you didn't,' she sighed. 'When will I learn not to take you seriously?'

'Never, I hope. I get a lot of laughs out of you,' he added.

'Thanks! For a lawyer you're pretty flippant. Nothing at all like Mr Seymour,' she added mockingly.

'Professional etiquette prevents me from passing comment on James Seymour.'

Callie giggled. 'In other words, you found him as much of an old misery as I did, but your professionalism stops you from agreeing with me.'

'Something like that,' Bill acknowledged.

'A typical noncommittal answer!'

'Lawyers are meant to be noncommittal.' He

swallowed the last of his whisky before standing up. 'I was going to ask you to spend Christmas with us, but in the circumstances . . .' he gave a knowing wink. 'Well, here's one Father Christmas who'd better be on his way. Marilyn's more excited than Paul is,' he revealed indulgently.

'Paul is still too young to understand.'

'Edith is convinced he knows exactly what's going on.' He raised his eyes heavenwards. 'Grandmothers!'

'I'm sure yours doted on you too.' Her eyes were a warm brown.

'Probably,' he sighed. 'Have a nice Christmas, Callie. And don't do anything I wouldn't.'

'There's no answer to that!'

'I'll take that as a compliment,' he grinned.

'Typical male!' she tutted. 'Give my love to Marilyn. And a hug for Paul.'

'I will.'

Callie set about putting the tree up in a bucket once Bill had gone. When she had looked at it in the shop the tree had looked perfect, but once in her flat it looked much too big, reaching almost to the ceiling.

As usual she had trouble finding the decorations, finally running them to earth in Jeff's studio. She spent a few minutes in the room that had been totally his, feeling close to him, seeking his approval of the man she was going to marry. The room felt warm, comforting, almost as if Jeff did actually show her he approved. Jeff had believed that no human being should be alone, that alone you died. Yes, Jeff would have approved of her marrying Logan, would have liked the other man's strength, his confidence. She left the studio with a feeling of well-being.

She had never felt so happy in her life, so breathlessly alive, wanting to shout her happiness to the whole world. Oh, it was going to be a wonderful Christmas, the best she had ever had!

CHAPTER SIX

SHE had already partly decorated the room when Logan arrived shortly before ten, suddenly feeling shy as she opened the door to him.

'Very seasonal!' He laughingly picked a piece of green-coloured tinsel from her hair, and bent to kiss her lightly on the nose. 'Happy Christmas, darling.'

'And you. Oh, Logan . . .!' She looked up at him with love-filled eyes, suddenly feeling tearful, suddenly feeling too much happiness at once.

'Let's go inside,' he groaned, leaning back against the closed door to pull her roughly into his arms, his mouth devouring hers with a fierce passion. 'I missed you today,' he murmured into her hair.

'I missed you too.' Callie trembled in his arms.

His eyes darkened as he looked down at her youthful beauty, smoothing the straight golden hair from her face. 'You look like a child,' he muttered.

She smiled at him. 'But I don't act like one,' she provoked.

'No.' He gave a husky laugh, his arm about her shoulders as they went through to the lounge. 'I see you've started.'

He looked appreciatively at the decorations she had already managed to put up.

'Mm, but I couldn't reach the corners.'

For the next half hour they finished putting up the paper chains, holly and mistletoe, although the latter proved to be uproarious, as Logan insisted on kissing her every time she pinned a piece of mistletoe to a picture or door.

'Stop it, Logan!' she finally giggled.

He moved to attach a piece of the green, cream-fruited bush to the light-fitting. 'Now there's nowhere in the room you can go without my being able to kiss you,' he said with satisfaction, very relaxed in a light grey shirt and black trousers, his black jacket discarded in a chair.

'Except the tree,' Callie taunted, pulling out the box of decorations to begin hanging the gaily coloured baubles on the lush green branches.

Logan looked at the tree admiringly. 'Did you carry this in yourself?' he frowned.

'Yes,' she glanced round at him. 'Why?'

'It looks heavy——'

'It was.' She moved to stand beside him, her arm about his waist.

'You could have hurt yourself.' His arm tightened about her shoulders.

'But I didn't,' she placated, kissing him on the cheek. 'Come and help me decorate the tree.'

'Then can I give you your present?'

She blushed at the warmth in his grey eyes. 'Yes,' she answered huskily.

'Right,' he said briskly. 'Let's get the tree done quickly.'

It looked really beautiful when they had finished, the coloured lights shining through the tinsel they had draped over the whole tree.

Callie's eyes glowed as she looked around the room. 'It all looks beautiful,' she said excitedly. 'Oh, Logan, I can't tell you what having you here means to me! I— I thought I was going to be alone, and it—it would have been the first time that had happened.' She looked down at her hands. 'As a child I had my parents, then Mummy, and then Jeff.'

'The man who died?'

'Yes,' she swallowed hard.

'You still miss him?'

'Just a little,' she nodded. 'He—he meant a lot to me.'

'I can see that,' Logan said huskily.

She gave a bright smile. 'You can have your present now. I'll just go into the bedroom——'

'Exactly where I wanted to go.' He moved purposefully towards her.

'Logan!' Callie looked at him with wide eyes. 'I meant your present is in there.'

'Yes.' His eyes brimmed with laughter.

'Will you behave!'

'Do I have to?'

'No,' she sighed her defeat, and moved into his arms, her face raised invitingly.

For long moments he was tempted. 'No,' and he finally put her away from him, 'it wouldn't be a good idea.'

Callie pouted her disappointment. 'I was only teasing.'

'I wasn't.' He relaxed in one of the armchairs. 'Off you go.'

'Logan Carrington, you——'

'Yes?' he raised one eyebrow.

'Nothing,' she snapped. 'I'll get your presents.'

Logan had taken advantage of her absence to go down to his car, and five parcels waited for her on the coffee-table, one of them almost the size of the table itself.

Callie frowned as she looked down at it. 'What on earth is that?'

'Open it and see,' he laughed.

'You open yours first.' She handed him his parcels, feeling a little awkward, hoping that he would like them.

She had bought him a ridiculously extravagant robe in pure silk, a contrasting cravat, a large bottle of the aftershave he usually wore, and of course the cufflinks. His pleasure at all of the gifts was genuine, and she knew she had chosen well.

'Now you,' he invited. 'And save that big one until last.'

'Spoilsport!'

'Go on,' he laughed.

Logan's gifts were even more extravagant than her own, a huge bottle of her favourite perfume, a large box of chocolates, a nightgown and négligé in the sheerest white silk she had ever seen.

'For our wedding night,' he told her softly.

'It's beautiful!' Her voice was husky.

'Now this one,' and he held out a flat square parcel.

Callie ripped the paper off, looking down at the jewellery box with wide eyes, undoing the clasp with shaking fingers. Inside, on the royal blue velvet, nestled a beautiful gold and diamond necklace.

She looked at Logan with disbelieving eyes. 'For me?'

'Well, it certainly isn't for me,' he drawled.

'Oh, Logan!' she threw herself into his waiting arms, kissing him with more exuberance than accuracy. 'I love you!'

'I should hope so,' he teased, his grey eyes twinkling with amusement. 'I don't think I'd approve of your kissing any other man like that.'

She nuzzled against his chest. 'Only you, darling. Only ever you.'

'Open the big present now,' he encouraged. 'I think you'll like it.'

'You've given me too much already,' she protested.

'The last one is for fun. Go on, open it.'

She looked up at him uncertainly. 'You aren't mocking me in any way?'

'No, little one,' he spoke gently, 'I'm trying to please you.'

The huge pink fluffy elephant she unwrapped did please her, so much so that she cried.

'He's perfect,' she hugged the toy to her. 'Just perfect!'

'He?' Logan mocked.

'Oh yes,' she gave him a mischievous smile. 'He's going to sleep with me, share my bed, until you do.'

His eyes darkened, desire in their depths. 'You only have to say the word,' he moaned raggedly.

'We have to face your mother, remember?' she teased.

'Do you think I care about my mother at this moment?'

'Really, Logan!' she pretended to be shocked. 'Not in front of Dumbo!' She pulled the grey ears over the pink face.

'Dumbo!' he scorned.

'I loved that film, did you?'

He looked deliberately blasé. 'I think I may have seen it in my youth.'

'Oh yes?' she mocked.

'Yes. Really, Callie, I'm not sure I can take the transition from Charlotte Brontë to Walt Disney,' he taunted.

Her happiness instantly faded, and the light died from her eyes. 'I'm too young for you.' She bit her lip.

'Like me to prove you're wrong?'

She swallowed hard, wanting to be the adult he wanted, that he needed. 'Yes,' she answered firmly.

'Like to belong to me?'

'Yes.' Her head went back proudly.

'Sure?'

'Yes——' This last affirmative came out in a sigh, and her head lowered as she looked at her hands.

'Then so you shall.' There was a movement behind her, and then Logan had joined her on the carpeted floor, taking the pink elephant out of her hands. 'For you.' He replaced the elephant with a small square jewellery box.

Her lashes flew upwards in surprise, searching Logan's face, finding none of the hardness she had seen seconds earlier. 'Is this—— Have you——'

'Open it.'

She did so with trembling fingers, and gasped at the emerald surrounded by diamonds—the most beautiful ring she had ever seen.

'Here, let me.' Logan took the ring from the box, discarding the latter on the floor and slipping the ring on the third finger of her left hand. 'Perfect,' he said with satisfaction, still holding her hand. 'Do you like it?'

'I love it!' Callie looked down at it in awe. 'But isn't it——'

'Perfect for my future wife,' he told her arrogantly. 'We can hardly be engaged without a ring, Callie.'

'I didn't know we were engaged.' She couldn't stop looking at the ring, sure it must have cost a small fortune.

'Only for a week or two.' His arms came about her. 'Just until we can arrange the wedding.'

'Won't everyone be shocked at the rush we're in?' She snuggled into his arms.

'They'll be even more shocked if we don't rush.' He chuckled as she blushed. 'I can hardly wait for the day you promise to love, honour, and obey me.'

'I shall have obey left out of the service,' she told him primly. 'You have to promise to worship me with your body,' she reminded shyly.

'I already do.'

She suddenly felt as if she had too much, as if something were going to happen to take her happiness away from her, and she couldn't repress the shiver of apprehension.

'What is it?' Logan was instantly sensitive to her mood, looking down at her. 'Callie?'

'You won't ever leave me, will you?' She clung to him. 'I think I'd die without you now.'

'You silly child——'

'I'm not a child! I'm really not, Logan.' She looked at him fearlessly.

'No, I don't believe you are,' he said slowly. 'And you'll never lose me, Callie, I can promise you that.' His arms tightened about her. 'I have too much to lose.'

His lips covered hers as they clung together, Logan's hands caressing, cupping one of her breasts, his thumbtip finding the erect nipple.

Callie could feel his full arousal against her thigh, and a weakness invaded her own limbs as his hand moved beneath her loose top to touch the nakedness of her breast, to caress the silky skin.

'I want to make love to you, Callie,' he groaned.

She knew that, knew that with every fibre of her body; a primitive force was driving him onwards tonight as he demanded her full submission. And she wanted to submit, denying them both at the cost of much pain to herself.

'We have to wait, Logan,' she breathed softly. 'We have to wait.'

'Do we?' He looked down at her with dark eyes. 'Yes, we do,' he sighed, helping her to her feet. 'We'll just have to make the wedding soon,' he attempted lightness. 'And damn what everyone thinks.'

She looked at him seriously. 'You don't think I'm being—silly? That I——'

'No,' he denied forcefully, clasping her upper arms. 'You aren't being silly at all. And I'm sorry if I upset you earlier. I was only teasing you.'

'Were you?' She wasn't so sure.

'Yes,' he smiled. 'I love your ability to enjoy a variety of things in life.'

'Jeff always said——'

'I'm beginning to hate the sound of that name,' Logan rasped, frowning darkly.

'No!' she gasped.

'Yes,' he insisted grimly. 'You're forever quoting the man. I'm the one you're supposed to love——'

'And I do,' she said fervently.

'Then stop talking about him as if he were some damned god, whose every word was immortal!'

'I'm sorry,' she whispered in a choked voice. 'It was just that I loved him, you see. And——'

'And he's dead!' Logan scowled. 'I'm the one that's alive. Remember that.'

'Yes.' She swallowed hard, finding it impossible to respond to his hard goodnight kiss.

As she lay in bed that night she was full of uncertainties. Oh, not about her love for Logan, that was unshakeable, undeniable. But how well did she know this man she loved? Would she *ever* understand him?

Logan still seemed as grim when he called for her the next morning, and the drive to his mother's home was made in total silence, Callie shooting nervous glances beneath lowered lashes in his direction.

Finally she couldn't stand it any longer. 'Logan——'

'Callie——'

They both began talking at the same time, and now she ruefully invited Logan to talk first.

'I'm sorry,' he said abruptly.

'Sorry . . .?' Her eyes were wide, the gold flecks in the brown more noticeable.

'Yes,' he nodded tersely. 'I behaved like a fool last night.'

She couldn't deny it. Logan had behaved badly, had acted jealous of a dead man. Jeff had never hurt anyone while he was alive, he certainly couldn't hurt anyone now he was dead.

Logan gave her a sideways glance. 'Do you still want to marry me?' He was gripping the steering-wheel so tightly his knuckles showed white.

Her hand moved to rest on his thigh. 'Of course,' she answered without hesitation.

'Oh, Callie!' he pulled the car over to the side of the road, turning in his seat to look at her. 'You're sure?'

'I never doubted it,' she replied with certainty. 'Maybe you've changed your mind?' Her breath caught in her throat as she waited for his answer.

'Not for a moment.'

Her breath left her in a sigh. 'That's all I needed to know. I won't talk to you about Jeff again—'

'No!' he shook his head. 'He was important to you, I have no right to deny you to talk about him.' He pulled her into his arms. 'Maybe you could just not do it too often, eh?' he added ruefully.

'I won't,' she said happily, raising her face for his kiss.

Logan drew back with a sigh, resting his forehead on hers. 'I must have spent the worst night imaginable.'

'No, I did that.' Her fingertips gently touched his hard cheek.

'God, I'm a fool,' he groaned. 'I think I've always been possessive. Maybe it comes from being an only child, but anything that's important to me I find impossible to share.'

Callie frowned. 'But Jeff could never have hurt you. He——'

'No more, Callie,' he put gentle fingers over her lips. 'It's Christmas, we're newly engaged, so no more arguments. This last one nearly killed me,' he admitted raggedly.

Such pain merited a kiss, two kisses, three kisses, so many kisses that when they slowly moved apart they were both breathless.

Callie gazed up adoringly into Logan's harsh features softened by love. 'I hate to spoil the moment,' she murmured softly. 'But what time is your mother expecting us for lunch?'

'Lord, yes!' He straightened in his seat. 'Thanks for reminding me.' His gaze was caressing as he started the car. 'The necklace looks nice, by the way.'

'So do the cufflinks,' she said shyly. It had given her intense pleasure to know that the cufflinks he wore with the light blue shirt were the ones she had bought for him.

They were laughing together when they entered Mrs. Carrington's house half an hour later, Callie once more secure in Logan's love.

But shyness overcame her at the thought of meeting her future mother-in-law. 'Do I look all right?' she asked anxiously.

'Beautiful.'

'Seriously, Logan——'

'Seriously, Callie,' he teased. 'You look beautiful. That silky thing is perfect.'

'That silky thing' happened to be a tan and brown suit that fitted smoothly over her slender figure, the high heels on her sandals adding height and giving her confidence. Her hair gleamed cleanly golden, the fringe winged back, the rest hanging straight to her shoulders.

'If you're sure?' She was still nervous. The housekeeper who had opened the door to them was daunting to say the least, although Logan greeted her familiarly enough.

'I'm sure,' he smiled, her hand held firmly in his. 'I can't wait to see my mother's face when she sees you.'

An elderly woman rose from the chair next to the fire, her grey hair softly permed, grey eyes twinkling kindly in the linked powdered face. Mrs. Carrington was no taller than Callie, although age had given her a regal bearing, and her figure was still petite; she was wearing a 'silky thing' herself, in blues and greens.

'Logan!' she greeted her son with obvious warmth, receiving his kiss on the cheek with a similar gesture.

Logan pulled Callie forward as she hung back shyly. 'Mother, this is Callie Day—my fiancée.'

His mother looked startled, surprised, but most of all, overjoyed. 'Welcome to the family, my dear,' she said warmly, kissing Callie on the cheek. 'Goodness, this is a happy day for me,' she said cheerfully. 'I thought Logan would never get married!'

His arm was possessive about Callie's waist. 'One look at this young lady and I was lost,' he told his mother cheerfully.

'You weren't so pleased at the time,' Callie teased, at once feeling at ease. There was none of the resentment from Mrs. Carrington that she had heard about in other mothers where their sons were concerned.

'No,' he gave a throaty laugh. 'But I am now.'

'This calls for champagne!' His mother's face glowed with excitement. 'Logan, ring for Kath and then we can toast the two of you.'

'Champagne at twelve-thirty, Mother?' he mocked, ringing for the housekeeper.

'For breakfast if we want it,' his mother refused to be daunted. 'Oh, Logan, you couldn't have given me a nicer Christmas present!'

It was the perfect opportunity for Callie to give Mrs. Carrington the roses and cut-glass vase, and she in return received a bottle of Chanel from the other woman.

'I had no idea the friend Logan was bringing with him was going to be my daughter, or I would have bought you something more personal.' The elderly woman arranged the roses in the vase while the housekeeper left to get the champagne. 'And talking of families . . .' she was looking out of the window into the driveway now.

'Oh, Mother, you haven't!' Logan groaned, closing his eyes.

Mrs Carrington looked flustered now. 'It's traditional, Logan, you know that. They always come to me for lunch on Christmas Day.'

'Yes,' he sighed his displeasure. 'It's the one tradition I always disliked.'

'Logan, behave yourself!' he was told sternly. 'I know you don't like them, and they know it too, but please just for once try to behave yourself.'

Logan joined Callie on the sofa, scowling darkly. 'God, I'd forgotten they'd be here,' he muttered. 'If I'd remembered we wouldn't have come. Lord, they're all I need!' he finished disgustedly.

Callie was no longer listening to him, her eyes widening with shock as she recognised Sir Charles and Lady Spencer, the anaemic Donald following them into the room.

'This is—is your family?' she choked.

He nodded, still scowling. 'My aunt, uncle, and weak-kneed cousin Donald.'

Callie felt as if she were going to faint, paling even more as Lady Spencer instantly recognised her.

'You!' she gasped, her expression as horror-struck as Callie's own must be.

'Good God!' Sir Charles stared at her in disbelief.

'Caroline . . .?' Donald frowned.

She slowly stood up, swaying as she did so. Christmas had suddenly turned into a nightmare, one she might never come out of.

Logan stood up too, his arm coming about her waist. 'You've already met my fiancée?' he said slowly.

'Fiancée?' Lady Spencer echoed shrilly. 'You mean you're going to marry this—this person?'

His eyes became steely. 'Yes, I am. What does it have to do with you?'

'Logan!' his mother begged pleadingly.

'I'm sorry, Mother,' he said tautly. 'But Aunt Susan is being rude about Callie, and I——'

'Caroline,' his uncle corrected angrily. 'Caroline Day.'

'Yes,' Logan nodded, waving Kath away as she arrived with the champagne. The woman left with a puzzled frown.

'Very clever of you, my boy,' his uncle snapped. 'I could have sworn your lack of interest that day in my office was genuine. I had no idea you intended taking up your idea yourself.'

Logan gave an impatient sigh. 'What idea?'

'Why, to marry Caroline and keep the shares in the family.'

'No . . .!' Callie moaned, pain shooting through her body. 'Oh no, not Logan!'

'What the hell is going on?' he rasped. 'Callie——'

'Caroline,' she corrected shrilly. 'My name is Caroline Day, as you've known all the time.' She wrenched away from him.' 'How could you, Logan? How could you?' she choked, her eyes huge in her pale face.

Logan was the person behind Donald's desire to marry her for the shares in Spencer Plastics, just as Logan himself had set out to marry her for the same reason. She had thought a warped mind was behind the scheme, now she knew it had to be true. Everything Logan had ever said to her was a lie, every word of love had been a lie, their whole engagement was a lie.

She drew off the engagement ring and held it out to

him, surprised at her own control. 'I won't be needing this any more.' Her voice was brittle.

Logan looked at her with dazed eyes. 'You're going to marry me. You said you were,' he finished lamely.

'And if your mother hadn't invited your uncle and aunt I probably would have done,' she said bitterly. 'For that I thank you, Mrs Carrington,' she looked at the elderly woman, her head held high. 'You can have no idea what you've saved me from. I know you weren't involved in this—this desception,' her voice softened. 'Jeff always spoke of you so lovingly.' She now knew that Logan's mother was the sister Jeff had admired so much, that Logan's mother was 'Cissy'.

'Jeff?' Logan echoed sharply. 'You can't mean this Jeff you're always talking about was my Uncle Jeffrey?'

She gave him a scornful look, her heart breaking inside at the way he had deceived her, at how he was still trying to deceive her. 'Stop pretending, Logan,' she said hardly. 'I know the truth now, so you can stop the act.'

'The truth? But I—— You're the woman who lived with my uncle?' His eyes had narrowed to icy grey slits.

'You know I am!'

'I think it's too bad of you, Logan, to try and get control of Spencer Plastics in this way,' Donald reproved.

'Shut up, Donald!' his cousin rasped, running a hand through his dark hair, for once not his immaculate self.

'Donald's right,' his aunt put in waspishly. 'I think the way you've gone about this is very underhand.'

'Underhand!' Logan repeated disgustedly. 'As I

understand it, my dear cousin would have been only too happy to have achieved the same result.'

'Well—yes,' Donald flushed. 'But at least you knew about it. It was your idea, after all.'

'Yes, it was my idea,' Logan ground out, looking at Callie with bleak eyes. 'But I had no idea how young and beautiful Miss Day was.'

'And as soon as you did you decided to marry her yourself,' his uncle concluded. 'Really, Logan, you could have let us in on your plans.'

'And have you ruin it all?' he scorned.

'As they have now,' Callie said dully, each word Logan uttered cutting into her like a knife. He had seemed so genuine in his love, so much in love, and it had all been a sham. How he must have laughed at her easy capitulation, her girlish adoration of him. Well, she wasn't a girl any more, she had suddenly grown up, and if she had been determined to fight the Spencers she was ten times more determined to fight Logan.

'Yes,' he bit out, his eyes a cool grey, his jaw rigid. 'But for whom?' he questioned bitterly.

Callie frowned. 'What do you mean?'

'What indeed?' he drawled insultingly.

'You won't get away with this, Logan,' his uncle snapped. 'I have no intention of letting you gain control of Spencers.'

'Neither do I!' Callie told him vehemently.

Logan spoke to his uncle, but his gaze didn't waver from Callie. 'And why would I want Spencers? My own company is enough for me.'

'Men like you never have enough!' Callie said contemptuously.

'Men like me?' he repeated softly, dangerously.

'Power-hungry!' Her mouth curled back in a sneer.

'Well, *really*, my dear, there's no need to resort to insults,' Lady Spencer put in in her ultra-superior voice.

'Isn't there?' Callie scoffed. 'Believe me, I haven't even started yet.'

'On the contrary,' ice seemed to drip from Logan's voice. 'You're finished.'

'Logan——'

'Stay out of this, Mother,' he said dismissively.

'Yes, please do.' Callie spoke gently to the bewildered woman; most of the conversation was obviously going over her head. Jeff had been right to pick her out as his favourite; Cicely Carrington was completely without guile or avarice—unlike her son, who possessed cruelty and greed in full measure. 'I'm sorry this had to happen here,' she said softly. 'Jeff wouldn't have liked to have seen you hurt.'

'Jeff? You mean Jeffrey?' Mrs. Carrington was slowly catching up with the conversation. 'You mean my brother Jeffrey?'

'Of course, Cissy,' Sir Charles answered impatiently. 'Haven't you understood a word of what's been said?'

Although she was the elder of the two Cicely looked flustered by his brusqueness. 'Well, not really,' she stuttered. 'What does Jeffrey have to do with Callie and Logan?'

'Everything!' Logan declared with feeling.

'Oh, Cissy, do *listen*!' Lady Spencer was abrupt with her sister-in-law. 'Caroline is the girl who lived with Jeffrey until he died.'

'And where is Caroline now?' Cissy blinked her puzzlement.

'Here,' Callie told her quietly.

Cicely Carrington looked at her with light grey eyes, frowning deeply. 'But—but you can't be!'

'But I am.'

'No, my dear. You see——'

'Mother, I'll fill you in on the bits you missed later,' Logan interrupted tersely.

'Does this mean that you and Callie aren't getting married?' Disappointment showed in her face.

'Definitely not!'

'I'd rather be dead!'

The two of them had spoken at the same time, their denials equally vehement, and Logan's mouth tightened at Callie's answer. 'You're lucky you aren't already,' he rasped coldly.

'I'm not frightened of you,' she scorned.

'Then maybe you should be.'

The very coolness of his voice was what made her blanch. 'I'll go upstairs and get my things, then I'll leave. Merry Christmas, everyone,' Callie added cryptically, leaving the room with her head held high, waiting until she had closed the door before allowing her shoulders to slump, the tears to fall.

This morning she had been so happy, a false happiness as it turned out, and now her world had shattered into tiny fragments, fragments she didn't have the will or energy to even try to put back together.

There were raised voices coming from the drawing-room now, evidence that the Spencers were still annoyed at Logan's duplicity. He had been so clever—the apparently accidental meeting, giving up Danielle to go out with Callie as if she were special in his life, the no-touching approach that was intended, and had succeeded, in making her *want* him to touch her. Yes, she had fallen into the trap he set for her, had been a willing victim, and the price was a broken heart, and a lack of trust in anyone ever again.

There was still one thing she had to verify in this situation, the final nail in the coffin, so to speak, an idea brought about by something James Seymour, of all people, had said.

She had brought Bill's report on Spencer Plastics with her, not really wanting to leave a private documented file like that about her flat over Christmas. There was only one thing in that report that interested her, one piece of information that would damn Logan for ever in her eyes.

Yes, there it was, in Bill's neat handwriting—a list of the shareholders of Spencer Plastics. Herself, Sir Charles, and Cicely Carrington, and below the latter was the name of the person who controlled her shares for her, and that name was Logan Carrington.

She had thought Donald was 'the nephew' James Seymour spoke about with such dislike; now she knew it to be Logan. She hadn't thought it could be poor Donald, he was so innocuous no one could possibly take such a dislike to him!

'I'm glad you can still find something to smile about,' snapped a contemptuous voice.

Callie turned to face Logan, swallowing her nervousness, determined not to let him see how much he had hurt her. 'What do you want?' she asked rudely.

'To talk.' His mouth twisted. 'What else?' He came fully into the room and closed the door behind him, more threatening with every step he took towards her.

CHAPTER SEVEN

CALLIE stood up, stiff with contempt. 'I have nothing more to say to you,' she told him haughtily.

'Maybe not,' he scorned. 'But I have plenty to say to you.' His icy gaze levelled on the file she still held in her hand. 'And what would that be?' he taunted.

She gave a startled look. 'This? It—— Why, it—— Give it back to me!' she cried as he snatched the file away from her. 'How dare you!' she blazed.

'Didn't you learn anything about me, Call—Caroline?' His voice hardened over the latter. 'You should have learnt, even in our brief acquaintance, that I don't suffer fools gladly.'

'Meaning?'

'Meaning you're a fool.' He flicked slowly through the handwritten sheets in the file. 'You've done your homework thoroughly, I see.' He closed the folder with a snap and threw it down on the bed, thrusting his hand savagely into his trousers pockets. 'But not thoroughly enough,' he added contemptuously. 'You would have been better sticking with Donald,' he scorned. 'I know he doesn't have control of his shares yet, but it's only a matter of time, just until Charles dies or retires—although the latter isn't very likely,' he derided. 'But he would still have been a safer bet than me.'

Callie was very pale, shaking with reaction. 'I don't understand what you mean.'

'Like hell you don't!' Logan rasped. 'But I'd never

have let you take control of Spencer Plastics.'

'Take control . . .?'

'If you'd married me, *I* would have taken control, not the other way around!'

'Oh, I know that,' she scorned. 'It was a very clever plan, carried out with so much more finesse—and experience—than Donald ever could.'

Logan's mouth twisted. 'Don't try turning the tables on me, Caroline. I had no idea who you were until just now——'

'Don't lie to me!'

'Whereas it's obvious you knew all there was to know from the first.' His glance flickered pointedly over the file.

'No——'

'The evidence damns you, Caroline,' he scorned harshly. 'Your acting is superb—that degree of shyness you occasionally display was just the added touch needed to gain a man's interest. I fell for the whole thing, the whole damned act!'

'If anyone was acting it was you!'

'Give up, Caroline,' he sneered. 'The charade is over. I wouldn't marry you now if you gave me half your shares to do it.'

'And that I'll never do!' Her eyes blazed.

'Then it will have to be Donald after all. Don't worry,' he mocked harshly, 'he'll still be willing—Mummy and Daddy will make sure of that. Of course it's more long-term than marrying me would have been, but you would eventually have control. Donald certainly isn't strong enough to stop you.'

Callie stood up, her hands clenching and unclench-ing at her sides. 'Why are you twisting everything? Why try and make it look as if I'm the one who tried to trick you, when all the time you know you took over from Donald when you saw he wasn't going to succeed?'

'I didn't take over anything from my simpering cousin——'

'Of course you didn't,' she recalled bitterly. 'It was your idea in the first place, wasn't it?'

'What was?' Logan frowned.

'To marry me and——'

'If you say I wanted control of Spencer Plastics just once more I swear I'll hit you!' he ground out furiously.

'Hit away,' she challenged. 'It won't change the facts.'

'The facts as you're twisting them. Just tell me one thing, would making love to you have been part of the plan too if I hadn't said no?'

Callie swallowed hard, her cheeks colouring bright red. 'As you've just said, you were the one who said no,' she muttered, too embarrassed to look up.

'And that denial made you want me, didn't it?' he scorned.

'No——'

'Oh yes,' he gave a taunting smile. 'The rest of it may have been an act, your words of love a lie, but your response to me is genuine.'

Callie turned away. 'That's a lie! Having you touch me makes my skin crawl,' she told him with more vehemence than truth.

'Does it?' he scoffed, coming forward with determined strides. 'We'll just put that to the test, shall we?'

Her eyes were wide with fear as he pulled her hard against him. 'No!' She pummelled her fists on his shoulders and chest as he lowered his head to grind his mouth down on hers.

The contempt he felt for her was a tangible thing, and not for a second did she respond. Then his savagery turned to subtle seduction, his mouth tasting hers, his hands caressing her back and waist, leaving her trembling and wanting more by the time he drew back.

His eyes were like chips of ice as he looked down at her, thrusting her completely out of his arms as she would have leant weakly against him. 'Is your skin crawling now?' he taunted.

'I——'

'Don't attempt to lie again, Caroline. You may not want to, but you like what I do to you.'

She licked her lips nervously, knowing it would be useless to deny it. 'So?' she challenged.

'So did you like it when my uncle touched you too?'

She stiffened. 'Jeff?'

'Yes—Jeff,' he drawled. 'Quite a philosopher, my uncle.'

She flushed. 'He was worth ten of you!'

'So you did like it when he touched you,' Logan rasped.

'I don't understand——'

'How long did you live with him?'

'About four years. But I knew him for a couple of years before that.'

'That would make you sixteen when you met?'

'About that, I suppose,' she nodded, frowning.

'My God!'

Callie still frowned her puzzlement. 'What does my age have to do with anything?'

'Not a lot. I just had no idea that that twenty-two-year-old façade hid a woman of forty!'

'I beg your pardon?'

'Never mind,' he dismissed angrily. 'Didn't it bother you that my uncle was twenty-three years older than you?'

'Bother me?' she queried.

'Obviously not,' he rasped. 'And to think I imagined myself a good judge of character,' he added disgustedly.

Callie flinched as if he had hit her, knowing that the insult was meant for her—even though she had no idea why he had said it! In fact, half of this conversation was a puzzle to her.

'This time you weren't so clever, were you?' she snapped.

'No. And for once I have something to thank Charles for, although he doesn't realise it.'

'Because he knows the truth,' Callie said angrily. 'He knows you were the one who thought of marrying me to get those shares, that you were the one who decided to carry out that plan.'

Logan took a threatening step towards her, his expression savage. 'I warned you——'

'That you'd hit me?' she faced him fearlessly. 'Well, go ahead! But it won't do anything but increase my contempt for you.'

'*Your* contempt for *me*?' he echoed scathingly. 'And what about my contempt for you? God, I thought you were too young for me, but the thought of you with my uncle—It sickens me!'

Callie gasped. 'Jeff and I——?'

'Yes!' Logan snapped. 'Was it worth it, Call—Caroline? Did you enjoy being the mistress of a man old enough to be your father? Did you like it when he made love to you?'

She had gone a sickly grey colour, her breathing constricted in her throat. 'I—— You think that Jeff and I——'

'Oh, I don't think it—I know it. The whole family knew he'd been living with someone for the last four years.'

'Obviously none of you were interested enough to find out who with,' she said dully.

'I hadn't seen him since I was ten or eleven!'

'Maybe if you had, if you'd ever spoken to him, you wouldn't be such an arrogant bastard,' she gritted with dislike. 'I didn't live with your uncle——'

'You've already admitted that you did!'

'But not in the way you mean——'

'What other way is there?' he derided. 'Either you did live with him or you didn't.'

'I did. But——'

'But you didn't sleep together? Spare me that, Caroline——'

'My name is Callie,' she told him vehemently. 'It's always been Callie.'

'Except on an official basis then you're Caroline, like in a will.' He shook his head. 'Over the years, mainly because of my own experience with them, I've learnt not to trust women—any woman. But my uncle was certainly fooled by you. Was he very naïve, or just not very bright where you're concerned?'

The colour came and went in Callie's hollow cheeks. 'About as bright as you, I would have said,' she scorned, to hide her pain. Later she could allow herself to feel every stab wound Logan had given her. Now, at this moment, she wouldn't give him the satisfaction of knowing how he had misjudged her—

and his uncle. He could go on thinking these terrible things about Jeff and herself. Her love for him had died the moment she knew he was only using her, that his love meant nothing.

'Yes,' he rasped. 'But then I knew about you all the time, didn't I?'

'Oh yes!'

'Then I don't think there's any more to be said,' he told her distantly. 'I'm glad to say you haven't succeeded in your plan.'

'Haven't I?' she taunted coldly. 'As you said, there's always Donald. You and your uncle don't seem—on the best of terms,' she added mockingly.

'So?'

'I'm sure he would rather keep the shares in the family—*his* family.'

'You little——!' Logan thrust her away from him. 'God, you sicken me!'

'No more than you sicken me,' Callie said bitterly. 'So we're both agreed that we've had a lucky escape.'

'Without doubt.'

'Then let's just leave it at that, shall we?' She collected her bags together.

'Leave it?' he taunted grimly. 'Oh no, we won't leave it. But the next time we meet will be across a boardroom table. And believe me, you won't have things your own way then.'

'I never thought it for a moment.' Although that had been when she thought she just had Sir Charles to contend with, Logan was a much more formidable opponent.

And she was determined to fight now, she wouldn't let Jeff's memory be tainted in any way. Logan had told her exactly what the family believed about them, and that shocked her more than anything she had heard here today. Jeff had been of their flesh and blood, didn't they know him well enough to realise that he would never ever have contemplated the relationship they thought him guilty of? One day she would take great pleasure in telling them the truth, but not yet, not until they had known her full contempt.

'As long as you realise that,' Logan nodded arrogantly, and left the room as softly as he had entered it.

Callie was too numb to cry, too hurt, too bewildered—too damned mad! The arrogance of that family, to think they could say those things about Jeff and get away with it. For herself she was past caring, but for Jeff and——

'Caroline?' Donald Spencer hesitated in the doorway, his expression uncertain. 'Is it all right if I come in?'

'Why not?' she scorned, checking she had her handbag and case. 'I was just leaving anyway.'

'Ah. Well, I—I was wondering if you would like me to drive you home?'

His nervous eagerness jarred her nerves, but what he had just said reminded her of the fact that she had come here with Logan, that she no longer had transport home. 'You've only just arrived,' she pointed out stiffly.

'I don't mind.'

'But it's Christmas Day.'

'All the more reason for me to drive you home, there won't be any public transport today, and I doubt you'd get a taxi either.'

He was probably right, and yet she was loath to accept anything from this family; she disliked every member of it, with the possible exception of Cicely Carrington, who probably still hadn't caught up fully with the conversation. And yet what a triumph to leave with Logan's cousin, to show him that after all there *was* still Donald.

'Caroline?' he prompted hopefully.

'All right,' she accepted briskly. 'As long as we can leave now.'

'Oh yes, of course. Straight away.' He took the small suitcase out of her hand. 'Of course,' he repeated excitedly.

Callie walked down the stairs with her head held high, Donald trailing dog-like behind her, almost dropping her overnight case in his hurry to rush forward and open the huge double doors to the drawing-room.

'Thank you,' she nodded distantly, her eyes cold as her gaze passed slowly over every person in the room.

Cicely Carrington still looked totally confused, Lady Spencer looked irritated, Sir Charles looked glowering, and she looked lastly at Logan, meeting his open contempt with equal scorn. Not an hour ago she had thought him the most wonderful man in the world, had wanted to spend her whole life with him, and now she hated him with such a vengeance she would do anything she could to hurt him.

Lady Spencer's expression brightened as she saw Callie's case in her son's hand. 'You're leaving now, then?' she said in her aristocratic voice.

Callie's mouth twisted. 'Yes, I'm leaving. Donald has kindly offered to drive me.'

'Anyone care for a drink?' Logan cut in tautly, making straight for the drinks cabinet as no one answered him.

Callie watched with cold eyes as he poured himself a large glass of whisky, drinking it down in one gulp before refilling the glass.

'Isn't it a little early for that, Logan?' his mother frowned at him.

'A moment ago you were going to toast my engagement,' he reminded her grimly.

'But that was with champagne!'

'And now I prefer whisky,' he refilled the glass once again, seeming to feel nothing as he drank the fiery liquid straight down. 'I thought you said you were going, Miss Day,' he said rudely.

Callie flushed. 'I am. I just wanted to thank your mother——'

'Take it as said,' he rasped.

'Logan!' his mother gasped. 'I've never seen you behave like this before——'

'I'd never met Caroline before,' he scorned. 'You have to hand it to her, Mother, she's beautiful enough to drive a man to drink—or suicide.' His eyes darkened. 'I suppose Uncle Jeffrey's death was an accident? You hadn't found yourself a younger man, had you, Caroline?'

A red tide of anger passed over her eyes, and when it cleared four shocked faces and Logan's furious one, the red marks where her fingers had made contact with his face showing up clearly against his otherwise pale skin.

'You'll regret you ever did that,' he told her through gritted teeth.

'I don't think so,' she said coldly, her hand stinging from the force of the slap. 'Ready, Donald?'

'Er——yes.' He eyed his cousin warily.

Logan's expression was contemptuous. 'She'll eat

you for breakfast,' he sneered.

'Well, at least he might be asked to stay for breakfast!' Callie had the satisfaction of seeing Logan pale even more, a pulse working erratically at his jaw. 'I'll be seeing you again soon, Logan.'

'You certainly will,' he acknowledged tautly.

She was shaking by the time Donald helped her into the passenger seat of the Jaguar, adjusting the seat-belt for her before moving round to get in behind the wheel.

She stared straight ahead for most of the journey, too sickened by what had happened to want to talk to anyone, least of all the insipid Donald. For once he seemed to know how she felt, and wisely remained silent—although it couldn't last for long.

'I do think it was very bad of Logan,' he said when he finally couldn't contain himself any longer.

She looked at him with dull eyes, no joyous gold flecks in their depths. 'What was?'

'Well, tricking you in that way——'

'Wasn't it what you intended yourself?'

Donald flushed. 'Certainly not!'

She sighed. 'Too much has been said to lie now. You even admitted it earlier.'

'Well——yes.'

'Thank you. And in future I would prefer equal honesty.' She rubbed her temples wearily. 'There doesn't seem to have been much of that lately.'

'I say, Caroline,' he turned to frown at her, 'has Logan really hurt you?'

'No, of course not.' She straightened her shoulders. 'It was just a game—a game we both lost.'

'You don't have to lose,' he pointed out tentatively. 'There's still me.'

'Is there?' she said dully.

'Oh yes,' he nodded his eagerness.

Callie shook her head. 'I don't think so, Donald. Spencer Plastics is just going to have to take its chances between the three of us.'

Donald chewed on his bottom lip. 'My father isn't going to be very happy about that.'

She only just bit back her bitterness, not giving a damn about Sir Charles' happiness. 'Why?' she queried calmly.

'He wants to expand Spencer Plastics,' Donald confided.

'Yes?'

'Logan doesn't.'

'Oh.'

Donald eyed her curiously. 'He doesn't usually stand out against my father, but this time he has. How would you feel about the expansion?'

The need to hit out at Logan was strong, and yet she didn't know enough about the facts to hit out in this way. 'I'd need to know more about it before I passed any comment either way,' she answered evasively.

'I'm sure my father would be only too happy to explain to you.'

'Some other time, Donald,' she dismissed sharply.

'Maybe after the holidays?'

'Maybe,' she agreed noncommittally.

She heaved an inward sigh of relief as they turned into the road she lived in. London was curiously deserted on this overcast Christmas Day. It had to be the one day in the year when even England's capital ground to a halt.

'Thank you, Donald.' She hastily opened her door

and got out on to the pavement, the bitter-cold wind cutting into her.

He took her small case out of the boot. 'Like me to come up with you?'

'No! Er——no, thanks, Donald,' she erased the sharpness from her voice. 'Please go back and have your lunch.'

'I'd rather stay with you.'

She could believe he meant that. Christmas in the Carrington household didn't look like being much fun. 'Your aunt is expecting you, Donald,' she insisted. 'Call me after the holidays, will you?'

'I'd like that.'

She nodded dismissively, hurrying up to her flat. It all looked exactly as she had left it—the bright gaiety of the decorations and Christmas tree, her opened presents beneath the latter, the nightgown and négligé Logan had bought her lying mockingly in the box.

The first thing she did was pack up all the presents Logan had given her, including the necklace she had forgotten to return to him earlier. Everything would go back to him, she didn't want anything he had given her.

She lived the next few days in a haze, going to bed, getting up in the morning, switching on the television and dully watching the antics of celebrities who seemed to be perfectly normal the rest of the year.

She forgot all about eating, so that by the time Christmas was at last over she was pale and listless. She went into Jeff's studio a lot, the place where she felt closest to him. This studio had always been sacrosanct when Jeff was alive. It was very full at the moment, as he had been preparing for another exhibition, one guaranteed to be even more successful than the last.

Jeff didn't just make likenesses in clay, he made his subjects come alive; he had a rare sensitivity that incorporated a person's personality into the sculpture and not just a physical outline.

The one Callie loved the most stood in pride of position beside his work-table, set there to give Jeff encouragement in times of lack of inspiration. And as he had been a true artist, a genius, there were all too many of them.

The subject was a woman, the whole figure no more than two feet long, the form of a sheet draped over the lower half of the body, the waist slender, the breasts full and uptilting, the neck slender, the face so beautiful, so without pain or suffering, that just to look at it made Callie want to cry.

It was her mother who lay there so serene, shown through the eyes of the man who had loved her, who had married her, even though they had both known she was dying. Jeff had been married to her mother, had been her stepfather, and when her mother had finally died six months ago Jeff had seemed to lose the will to live too. Oh, not that Callie thought for one moment he had deliberately killed himself, he just hadn't wanted to live, wanted only to join her mother.

Her mother had been very like her to look at, but there had been lines of pain in her mother's face that made her seem older than her years. But Jeff had loved her unfailingly, had never ceased to hope that a cure could be found for her before it was too late, insisting on taking her to specialist after specialist at first, until, like her mother, he had become resigned to her death.

When he had first come into their lives almost six years ago her mother had tried to repulse him, had been deliberately hurtful at times, but Jeff had remained adamant about wanting to marry her, and had more or less camped on their doorstep. Finally her mother had relented enough to allow him to spend time with them. But it still wasn't enough for Jeff—he wanted marriage, and nothing else would satisfy him. Her mother had been so confused, she had wanted to marry him, and yet didn't think it fair that Jeff should be marrying a woman who was dying. In desperation she had finally asked Callie what she should do, and Callie's reply had been unreserved.

The three and a half years her mother had been married to Jeff had been some of the happiest for them all, some of the saddest too. It became a game to Jeff to think up new ways to entertain her mother, especially towards the end when she was bedridden.

Jeff's family had obviously never been told about the marriage, and wouldn't know that it had been another Caroline Day, her mother, who had been the woman Jeff loved, the woman he lived with, the woman he married.

But they would pay for their degradation of a love that had been so pure and beautiful that Jeff and her mother might have been teenagers loving for the first time. And Logan would pay the most.

'Can I come in?'

Callie swung round at the sound of his voice, knocking the stand in front of her, the sculpture of her mother falling, as if in slow motion, towards the floor. But it never made contact; Logan's reflexes were quicker than her own as he caught the sculpture inches from the ground.

'I knocked,' he told her abruptly, looking closely at the figure in his hand, 'but you didn't hear me.'

'No.' She snatched the sculpture out of his hand and put it back on the stand. Then she stood up, running her hands down her denim-clad thighs. 'What do you want?' she asked coldly.

His eyes were narrowed to grey slits; he was wearing a sheepskin jacket over a sweater in the cold of the day, looking big and powerful, droplets of melting snow in the darkness of his hair. Callie noticed everything about him at a glance, feeling a familiar stirring of her senses, a feeling that she instantly dampened.

He moved to stand beside the sculpture. 'I came to see if I might not have misjudged you,' he murmured slowly, seemingly mesmerised by the sculpture of her mother. 'I don't think I have.' His eyes were raised accusingly.

Callie looked at the sculpture too, seeing what Logan must see—a sculpture of herself! Jeff had shown her mother as she was to him, still beautiful, with none of the suffering etched into her face. That Logan saw the sculpture as being her, Callie, she had no doubt.

'Good, isn't it?' She looked tauntingly up at Logan.

'Very,' he agreed tightly. 'Very lifelike.' One of his hands moved suggestively over the uptilting breasts.

'Stop that!' Callie angrily slapped his hand away. 'How dare you?' She glared up at him with tear-filled eyes.

His mouth twisted. 'Considering I've touched the real thing I'm surprised at your outrage,' he taunted.

'You may have touched the real thing, Mr Carrington,' she told him haughtily, 'but you never touched the real me.'

'Didn't I?' he challenged sceptically.

'No,' she stood her ground. 'When you've been loved by an expert an amateur can only ever be second-best.'

'Is that so?' His eyes glittered dangerously.

'Yes.' She gave him a considering look. 'You look very like Jeff in some ways, you know.'

She hadn't realised it before, but he did in fact have a look of his uncle about him—the same thick dark hair, a powerfully built physique, piercing eyes, although in Jeff they had been a deep blue. There was even a similarity about the features, although in pure good looks Logan had the advantage.

'You might even have liked him,' she added thoughtfully.

'I doubt it,' Logan snapped, frowning suddenly. 'This work looks familiar.' He picked up another of the sculptures, an old man bowed down by years of hard work. 'Thornton, right?'

'Right,' she acknowledged tightly.

'You know him?'

'I did.'

'So my uncle hasn't been the only man in your life,' he said accusingly.

'Don't be ridiculous,' Callie snapped. 'Jeff Thornton was your uncle!'

His eyes widened. 'My uncle did this?' He carefully replaced the sculpture on its stand.

'Yes.' She moved pointedly to the door, waiting for him to leave.

Logan took the hint, following her through to the lounge. 'I had no idea my uncle was so talented.'

'You knew nothing about him at all, so why should you know that?' she scorned.

'Did you pose for that sculpture?' he demanded to know, not answering her question.

'No,' she told him truthfully.

'Then he did it from memory. Is it for sale?' he rasped.

Callie paled, seeing his intention. 'Not for all the money you possess!' Her tone was vehement.

His mouth twisted. 'I wasn't going to offer that much. And I doubt you need it. I believe my uncle left you quite a rich young woman?'

'Yes,' she confirmed tightly.

'It was a good idea to keep on with your job, to continue living here, otherwise I might have become suspicious.'

'And it was a good idea of yours not to let me meet any of your family,' she derided. 'I *would* have been suspicious.'

Logan sighed. 'I thought we'd dropped the act.'

'I have—*you* haven't!'

'I'm not going to stand by and see you get control of Spencer Plastics!'

'The same applies to you.'

'God, this is ridiculous——'

'I couldn't agree more,' she said tightly. 'I thought we'd agreed that the next time we met would be at the shareholders' meeting?'

'When you will no doubt back Uncle Charles' plans to expand the company,' he snapped impatiently.

She shrugged. 'I may do.'

'Then you'll have nothing. Spencer Plastics can't handle the expansion he proposes.'

Callie was sure Logan knew a lot more about business matters than she did, but surely Sir Charles knew what was best for his own company?

'My uncle Jeffrey opposed it,' Logan put in softly.

Her eyes widened. 'Jeff did?'

'Yes. It came up at the last shareholders' meeting——'

'Which Jeff attended?' she frowned.

'No. He always had Seymour act for him. And he opposed it on his behalf.'

'Because Jeff didn't believe in capitalism,' she said instantly.

'And you do?'

'No . . .'

'Then you'll oppose it too?'

'I don't know.' She was becoming agitated now. 'I have to discuss it with Sir Charles.'

'And Donald?' he rasped.

'Probably,' she nodded haughtily.

'Don't you think I would make you a better husband?'

The colour came and went in her cheeks. 'No. I doubt you would make any woman a good husband,' she added bitchily.

'Maybe I should just become your lover?'

'Before or after I marry Donald?' Callie answered with a calm she was far from feeling.

She knew now that not all Logan's behaviour in the last few weeks had been a lie; his desire to possess her was still a tangible thing, his eyes were darkened with passion. Well, he was out of luck if he thought she would seriously consider an affair with him!

'That depends on when the wedding is to be,' he said grimly. 'Oh, soon, I think,' she said stiltedly, wondering if this situation could possibly get any worse. She had thought Logan had hurt her all he could, but these stab wounds were deeper than before.

'Then I'll wait until after the wedding.'

'And if I don't want you?'

'Are you saying you don't?' he derided.

'Yes,' she told him defiantly.

'I could easily show you differently.'

'You could try!'

Logan's eyes were narrowed. 'You would like that, wouldn't you?' he taunted.

'No——'

'Little liar!' he growled. 'It's over four months since my uncle died, you must be getting frustrated by now.'

Callie only just bit back her angry retort, refusing to rise to his obvious insult. 'There's always Donald,' she drawled.

Logan's expression was contemptuous. 'If you like to take the initiative.'

'Donald learns fast.'

'He would have to.'

Once again she had to hold back an angry retort. Had she really thought herself in love with this man? It seemed incredible now.

'If you've said all you came to say . . .' she said pointedly.

His gaze swept the flat—and her. 'And seen all I want to see,' he nodded.

'Then would you please leave?'

'Gladly,' he drawled.

'Take these with you.' She thrust his Christmas gifts at him.

He ignored them. 'I don't want them.'

'Neither do I!'

'Then give them away,' he shrugged, buttoning his jacket against the snow that had been falling since early morning, then pausing at the door to look down at her with darkened eyes. 'You know where to find me if you decide Donald isn't man enough for you.'

Callie leant weakly against the door. 'Will you just go?'

'Yes, I'll go,' he scowled, his hands rough as he pulled her towards him. 'But I'll make sure you don't sleep tonight either!' He ground his mouth down on hers, bending the fragility of her body into his as he ruthlessly plundered a response from her. When he at last raised his head Callie's legs felt boneless, so much so she had to cling to him for support. 'Yes,' Logan said with satisfaction, 'I think your night may be spent as sleeplessly as mine have been lately.' He put her away from him.

Callie regained control with effort, licking her lips to make sure they were still intact, feeling numbed from the force of Logan's. 'A guilty conscience has a way of doing that,' she told him vaguely.

'You should know,' came his parting shot.

She slowly closed the door as she heard the descent of the lift, leaning weakly back against the door to steady her nerves. Logan had been the last person she had expected to see today, to see ever again except in a business capacity. And the suddenness of seeing him had made her say things she would rather have left unsaid.

She moved to the telephone and dialled quickly, before she had time to change her mind. 'Donald Spencer, please,' she requested once the butler had answered the telephone. 'Donald? Call—Caroline here,' she amended. 'How about that meeting you suggested? Dinner tomorrow? Lovely,' she answered with false brightness, all gaiety leaving her once she had rung off.

CHAPTER EIGHT

'Good God, talk about the morning after . . .!' Mike eyed Callie mockingly the next day; the office was open once more, to her relief. Another day alone in her flat and she would have gone insane! 'I needn't ask if you had a good Christmas,' he teased.

'No,' she answered quietly, knowing she had never spent such a miserable time in her life as the last four days.

But she kept up the pretence all morning, only baulking when Mike asked if there were no boy-friend for lunch today.

'I thought this was *it*,' he teased her.

'No,' she evaded his eyes. 'It didn't work out.'

'Oh!'

'It's all right, Mike,' she told him brightly. 'I'm seeing someone else tonight.'

'Off with the old, on with the new?'

'That's right,' she laughed, hoping Mike wouldn't catch its rather hollow ring. He didn't seem to, and the rest of the day passed in a rush of work that she was grateful for.

Her heart leapt with pleasure when she got home later that night to find Marilyn and Bill back in their flat.

'I thought you were going to be away for months!' She hugged Paul to her, at once feeling better; his innocence was the balm she needed for her wounds.

Marilyn grimaced. 'Bill couldn't stand it any longer. Anyway, Dad's made a fantastic recovery. And I must say it's nice to be back in our own home.'

'It's good to have you back.'

Her friend frowned. 'Do I sense a little too much enthusiasm?'

Callie sighed, letting Paul climb down to play with his toys. 'You could do,' she admitted, knowing she couldn't bottle up the pain much longer. And Marilyn and Bill had been her friends for such a long time.

'Logan?' Marilyn prompted softly.

'Logan?' Bill echoed sharply as he came through from the kitchen.

'Yes,' Callie sighed. 'You may as well know the man I—the man I thought I loved was Logan Carrington.'

Marilyn still looked puzzled, but Bill wasn't quite so mystified. 'Carrington Cosmetics?'

'Yes.'

'Carrington shares in Spencer Plastics?'

'Yes,' she nodded miserably.

'The rotten, lousy——'

'Remember Paul!' she cautioned lightly.

Marilyn still looked completely in the dark. 'You've lost me, I'm afraid.'

Callie played on the floor with Paul while Bill explained to her friend.

'That's terrible,' Marilyn exclaimed in a shocked voice. 'He actually—He made you fall in love with him on purpose?' she gasped.

Callie nodded again. 'It seems that when it comes to business the Spencers and Logan have no holds barred.'

'Would you like me to go and give him a black eye for you?' Bill offered grimly.

It was very protective of him, very loyal, but she had an idea that, masculine as Bill was, Logan wouldn't be the one who had the black eye. 'I don't think so,' she laughed. 'Anyway, I've got my own back, I'm going out with his cousin tonight.'

'But isn't he as bad?' Marilyn frowned.

'But more harmless,' she smiled. 'Donald is just henpecked by his parents. Talking of which . . . Bill, someone mentioned expanding Spencer Plastics.' She gave him a querying look.

He shook his head. 'Not a good idea.'

'No?'

'Not in this financial climate. They would need a loan for the expansion, a loan with high interest rates, and probably little return for the next five years. If you've read the report——'

'I have,' she assured him.

'Then you'll know that at the moment they're making a substantial profit.'

'Mm.'

'With the expansion most of the profit would go to pay up the loan, there'd be nothing left for the shareholders. What is it?' he asked as he saw her grimace.

'Logan said something along the same lines.'

'Did he? Well, he's right. Of course, you're all rich enough to take such a loss, in the millionaire class,' he added teasingly. 'But there's no guarantee that you'll see a profit, even at the end of five years.'

'So no expansion?'

'I wouldn't advise it, no.'

'Damn,' Callie muttered.

'Why's that?'

'Logan didn't advise it either,' she revealed reluctantly.

'And you don't want to agree with him,' Bill nodded understandingly.

'No. I've also agreed to meet Sir Charles to discuss it over the weekend.'

'Well, I can't see any harm in discussing it. He may have a different idea for expansion from the one I've outlined. I doubt it, but it can't do any harm to talk to him.'

'Okay.' Callie stood up. 'I have to go and get ready for my date with Donald now. He may be an idiot,' she added ruefully, 'but at least now he's an honest idiot.'

'That's something!' Marilyn laughed.

Not even to Bill and Marilyn, her best and closest friends, had she been able to reveal the deep hurt she felt over the misinterpretation of Jeff and her mother's love for each other. That was somehow too personal to reveal to anyone.

Donald proved to be quite pleasant company later that evening, acting more naturally now that he didn't have the pretence of having to fall madly in love with her. Callie surprisingly enjoyed her evening with him, and found him to be very shy for his age, ridiculously eager to please, and quite lighthearted away from the dominating influence of his parents.

'My parents would like you to come to the family New Year party,' he told her on the drive back to her home.

She instantly stiffened. 'Will Logan be there?'

'He could be.'

She drew in a ragged breath. 'Then I think I'd rather not.'

'Oh, do come, Caroline,' he encouraged. 'Logan rarely comes to family parties, he doesn't really enjoy them. In fact, when I got back on Christmas Day he was rolling drunk. My mother was deeply shocked!'

She could imagine Lady Spencer had been. And the reason for Logan's drunken state was easily explained; his carefully laid plans had gone completely awry.

'My father thought you could have your little chat then,' Donald added, as if she couldn't possibly go against a suggestion his father had made.

'All right, Donald,' she smiled, wondering how anyone could remain so naïve with parents like his.

He turned and saw that look. 'I know what you're thinking,' he sighed. 'And so far I've done anything for a quiet life. But one of these days I'm going to turn around and surprise the lot of you.'

If he did Callie would lay odds on it being the first time he ever had!

The New Year party was well under way by the time Callie and Donald arrived at nine-thirty, although it wasn't the sort of party she was used to, with none of the boisterous music and loud chatter. Everyone stood around making intelligent conversation, diamonds dripping off the women, most of the men looking as if they had already had two coronaries and they were just waiting for their third.

'I'll get you a drink,' Donald suggested, back within seconds with two brimming glassfuls. 'Champagne,' he said boyishly.

What else? Callie thought cynically, glancing around

the room with studied casualness. No sign of Logan, although that didn't mean he wasn't going to come. After all, it was a welcome in the New Year party, so it would go on for hours yet.

'My dear Caroline!' Lady Spencer suddenly appeared at her side, a tall distinguished man at her side. 'Judge McCorley, I'd like you to meet my son's very dear friend Caroline Day,' she gushed.

'Glad to meet you, my dear,' the elderly man shook her hand warmly. 'Does this mean there will soon be wedding bells in the family?'

Lady Spencer's smile didn't waver by an inch. 'You never know, Malcolm, you just never know. Do you, Donald?' she gave her son a conspiratorial smile.

His smile wasn't so genuine. 'No, Mother.'

Lady Spencer put her hand through the crook of the Judge's arm. 'I'll take you round and introduce you to everyone else now, Malcolm. It's just that Caroline is—well, I thought it would be nice if you met her,' she gave a coy smile.

The Judge's look was openly speculative now, and Callie's smile was so fixed her face ached by the time the other couple left to circulate. She would have credited Lady Spencer with a little more subtlety than *that*!

'Mother is—Well, she—' Donald seemed at a loss for words. 'She has high hopes for me, maritally.'

Callie gave him a cool stare. 'And does the woman you love meet up to these—hopes?'

He flushed, his blue eyes guarded. 'I—You know you do.'

She put her hand comfortingly on his arm. 'Not me, Donald, the woman you *love*.'

'I——'

'And that isn't me. Is it?' she prompted.

He looked sheepish. 'No.'

She could almost have shouted with the triumph, the effort it had cost Donald to make that admission. 'You want my advice, Donald?'

'Er——' he frowned. 'Yes.'

'Marry the woman you love and forget everyone else.'

He sighed. 'It isn't that easy.'

'Believe me,' she squeezed his arm, 'it is.'

'Good evening, Donald—Caroline.' Logan's voice cooled over the last. 'I had a feeling you would be here.'

It took all her willpower to turn and look at him, her barriers momentarily down. He looked superb in a dark dinner suit, the snowy white shirt emphasising his tan, his eyes a cold metallic grey.

Callie drew a steadying breath, and answered with all the confidence she could. 'In that case I'm surprised you came.'

For a moment he didn't answer her, his gaze insolently stripping the rust-coloured dress from her body, lingering on the creamy expanse of skin left exposed by the single-shoulder fastening. And that was how he made her feel—exposed.

'This is a family party, Miss Day,' he told her abruptly. 'And I don't think you merit being called that—yet.' He waited for the barb to hit home before turning to the woman at his side. 'You both know Audrey, of course.'

Audrey Harris! Callie hardly recognised Logan's secretary in the body-hugging gold dress, her long black hair secured over one shoulder, her make-up vividly striking.

Donald frowned at the other woman. 'No, I——'

'It's Logan's secretary, darling,' Callie drawled, allowing the hand she had resting on his arm to move possessively against the fabric of his jacket, feeling a thrill of elation as Logan's eyes narrowed over the gesture. 'How nice to see you again, Miss Harris,' she said with false sweetness.

Violet-blue eyes narrowed speculatively. 'Miss Day,' Audrey drawled. 'Do let's go and meet someone interesting, Logan,' she added pointedly. 'You told me I'd have a good time, and so far it's been deadly dull.' Those violet-blue eyes returned challengingly to Callie.

Callie couldn't pretend she wasn't surprised to see Logan here with his secretary, especially after the derogatory remarks he had made about her, and yet in a way this encounter was amusing.

'I have a feeling I've played this scene before,' she mumbled.

'Not quite,' Logan mocked.

No, of course not. This time *she* was the discarded girl-friend. Well, she couldn't say she hadn't been warned!

'Could we go for a walk in the conservatory?' she asked Donald. 'The air is a little—stale, in here.'

Logan's mouth tightened at the jibe, his eyes snapping with anger. 'Come on, Audrey, let's find some of those interesting people I promised would be here.' They walked away, a very attractive couple, both tall, attracting much attention.

'The conservatory, Donald,' Callie reminded him jerkily as he still seemed awed by his impressive cousin.

'Oh, of course,' he agreed absently, walking towards

the back of the house where his mother nurtured her beloved roses. 'I don't know how Logan dare bring his secretary here,' he frowned. 'Mother will be furious when she finds out who she is. She can't stand the models he usually brings, let alone . . . Well, she isn't going to like it.'

Callie doubted whether it would bother Logan in the least what his aunt's opinion was on his bringing Audrey here, and she personally was weary of the bitchiness, the snobbery. She wished she had never agreed to come here, wished——

'Your mother wants you, Donald.'

She turned with a start at the sound of Logan's voice, her eyes widening as she saw he was alone. He was watching her with brooding eyes, making it impossible to tell what he was thinking.

'Mother does?' Donald frowned.

'Yes.' Logan looked coldly at his cousin. 'I should run along if I were you.'

'She wants me now?'

'Five minutes ago, I would say,' Logan taunted.

'Oh dear,' Donald looked hounded. 'Caroline——'

'I'll be fine, Donald,' she assured him.

'Come with me.'

'No, you go on.' She gave him a vague smile, having eyes only for Logan.

'Oh, but——'

'For God's sake go, Donald,' Logan snapped viciously. 'You aren't wanted here.'

'I say, Logan——'

'It's all right, Donald,' Callie soothed his hurt feelings. 'I'll join you in a minute.'

'Well—all right,' he gave in reluctantly. 'You understand? My mother——'

'Will you get the hell out of here, Donald!' Logan's expression was threatening.

Donald hastily left the heated room, closing the door behind him.

Callie gave Logan an angry look. 'That wasn't kind.'

'Neither is this game we're playing.'

'Game?' she blinked.

He shrugged. 'Well, it started out that way, it's more serious than that now.'

Callie moved away from the spell he was weaving about her, his magnetism seeming to draw her back again. 'I have no idea what you're talking about.'

He swung her round, retaining a hold on her upper arms so that she couldn't move away. 'No matter what the reasons for our first meeting, our engagement, we want each other now. Don't deny it, Callie,' he said as she went to speak. 'That you're using Donald, and I'm using Audrey, to shield that fact, can't change the truth.'

Her heart was beating so fast she thought it would deafen her, her breathing so shallow it seemed she hardly breathed at all.

'Did you sleep after I left you the other night?' he asked huskily.

The colour in her cheeks answered for her. She had suffered an agony of longing after he had left her, a need for him that he had meant to inflict.

'Your eyes tell me you didn't,' he smiled. 'And neither did I.'

She couldn't let him seduce her with these words, had to remember the way he had used her, deliberately made her fall in love with him. She also had to remember what he and his family thought of herself and Jeff.

'Does this mean you want the affair to start now?' she taunted. 'That *you* can't wait until after I marry Donald?'

His fingers bit into her arm. 'You aren't going to marry Donald.'

'Aren't I?' she challenged.

'No,' he ground out.

'Oh, but I am.' She wriggled out of his grasp. 'It's comforting to know you want me, Logan,' she mocked him. 'But you really are mistaken about me—I don't want you. Oh, no doubt you would be a satisfying lover, but I'm sure you wouldn't want to become my lover just because you remind me of Jeff?'

His expression was thunderous. 'You'll taunt me with him once too often!'

'And you've already played this scene once too often!' Her eyes flashed deeply brown. 'You've lost, why can't you accept that?'

'For God's sake forget the damned shares for a minute! I'm talking about you and me now,' he shook her.

'The only you and I there ever was is dead,' she told him dully.

'Callie——'

'Mother didn't want me at all, Logan,' a disgruntled Donald came back into the room. 'And your—Miss Harris is looking for you.'

Impatience warred with good manners in Logan. 'All right,' he sighed at last. 'I'm just going.'

As usual Donald seemed unaware of the friction around him. 'How's Aunt Cissy now?' he asked cheerfully.

Callie's gaze sharpened. 'Is your mother ill?' she asked Logan concernedly.

'She slipped in the snow the other night,' he informed her distantly.

No wonder she wasn't here tonight. 'I'm so sorry. Is she all right?'

'A little bruised, but otherwise fine,' she nodded.

'Father would like to talk to you now,' Donald told Callie eagerly. 'He's waiting for you in the library.'

'A little business discussion?' Logan drawled.

'And if it is?' she challenged.

'Then maybe I should be there too. Spencer Plastics is a three-way ownership, or have you forgotten?'

She shuddered. 'No, I haven't forgotten. But this is private, Mr Carrington.'

'In other words, mind my own business?'

'Yes!'

'Very well,' he turned on his heel, walking to the door. 'I'll see you on Thursday, Caroline.'

'Thursday?' she blinked.

'At the shareholders' meeting,' he drawled.

'Oh—oh yes,' she nodded. 'You'll be acting on your mother's behalf, as usual?'

'Of course,' he nodded arrogantly.

Callie felt less defensive once he had gone, turning to Donald with her composure back intact. 'Let's go and talk to your father.'

'Oh, he doesn't want me there,' Donald flushed. 'He never discusses business with me.'

'But surely—Never mind,' she dismissed, deciding that it was none of her business if Donald's father kept him excluded from business affairs.

It was the first time she had actually spoken to Sir Charles this evening, their few words of polite greeting not really counting as conversation. He was seated in one of the winged armchairs placed either side of the fire, a big cigar in his hand, a look of the cat-that-had-swallowed-the-cream about him. Callie suddenly felt as if she were the fly walking into the spider's parlour.

Sir Charles stood up as she hesitated in the doorway. 'Come in, Caroline,' he beamed. 'Come in. Sit down,' he invited.

She did so, taking a long time to arrange her skirts about her, looking up to surprise a contemptuous expression on Sir Charles' face, something he was quick to try and hide.

'Let's get straight to the point,' she said hardly. 'You want me to vote in favour of expanding Spencer Plastics. Why should I?'

'Well, I—I—You're a bit abrupt, my dear,' he spluttered in his booming voice.

'I like to be direct,' she pinpointed him with steady brown eyes. 'And I like people to be direct with me. So far I've heard all the arguments against, now I want to know your arguments for.'

That Sir Charles resented the necessity to confide anything to a chit of a girl was obvious over the next few minutes; his words were stilted and abrupt. By the time he had finished she was none the wiser, knowing nothing about the industry, despite having read Bill's in-depth file from cover to cover.

'Trust me, my dear,' Sir Charles encouraged at her totally bemused look. 'I've run my company for over thirty years, I hope to do so for another thirty.'

'Wouldn't you be rather—old, by then?' she frowned.

'In my prime, my dear, in my prime.'

'But surely Donald——'

'Doesn't have it in him, Caroline. Doesn't have it in him.'

It wasn't Sir Charles' annoying habit of saying everything twice that annoyed her the most, it was his brutal dismissal of his son's capabilities—even if he were probably right. Donald certainly wasn't the cut-throat material that seemed to be needed in a successful business. Look how far Logan had been prepared to go for the sake of business.

'I'll think about it.' She stood up.

'Not too long, my dear, not too long,' Sir Charles stood up too, dropping cigar ash all over the Persian rug. 'Meeting's in a few days. I need your support, Caroline.'

'I'll do my best.' She gave him a noncommittal smile.

'We'd better join the others now, it's a few minutes to twelve,' he opened the door for her. 'I've always liked the start of a new year—like a new beginning for everyone.' He walked away to join his wife.

A new beginning. Callie was beginning to think that was what she needed, a complete break from everything that reminded her of Logan. As the clock began to strike twelve she made that her resolution for the New Year. As soon as the meeting was over on Thursday she would go away on holiday.

'Happy New Year, Callie.'

She looked up into the face of the man she loved, would always love. 'Happy New Year, Logan,' she choked, her eyes full of tears.

His lips were feather-light on hers. 'Not exactly the

way I had envisaged us celebrating the New Year,' he said ruefully.

Her mouth tightened. 'No—well, even the best laid plans can go wrong.'

'Yes,' he sighed.

'I think Audrey is waiting for her own kiss.' She had caught a glimpse of venomous blue eyes. 'For the New Year, of course,' she added tauntingly.

'Of course,' Logan drawled.

'Happy New Year, Caroline.' Donald had joined them to sweep her into his arms to plant a wet kiss on her cheek.

The next few minutes were taken up with welcoming in the New Year, everyone kissing everyone else, and by the time Callie had a chance to look round for Logan he and Audrey had gone. Oh well, perhaps it was as well. She had started to feel a weakening in her resolve to keep him at a distance.

Bill accompanied her to the meeting on Thursday, his presence giving her confidence.

'Don't worry,' he assured her. 'Your vote counts as much as anyone else's.'

She straightened her shoulders, ready for the battle ahead. And she had no doubt there would be a battle.

They were shown into the boardroom by a rather busty-looking blonde in her early twenties, her blue eyes openly speculative as she showed them through.

Sir Charles and Logan were already seated at the long table when she and Bill walked in, and both men rose to their feet.

'Miss Day, Sir Charles,' the secretary told him.

'Thank you, Lena,' he dismissed. 'Please sit down, Caroline,' he pulled back a chair for her. 'Mr Lane,' he nodded abruptly.

'Thanks.' Bill sat next to Callie, putting a folder on the table in front of him.

'I don't think there was any need for your lawyer to be present,' Sir Charles chided Callie.

'Bill is also my business adviser,' she told him abruptly.

'Very well,' Sir Charles shrugged. 'Well, I suppose we might as well get down to business.'

'I haven't been introduced to Mr Lane,' Logan said sharply.

Callie's lids rose before fluttering down again, totally unnerved by how handsome he looked. 'Bill Lane, Logan Carrington,' she introduced abruptly.

'Bill?' Logan frowned. 'You wouldn't happen to have a little boy called Paul, would you?'

Bill was physically taken aback by the question. 'Why—yes,' he frowned.

'How is he?' Logan's concern was genuine, a smile of gentleness on his face. 'He was teething when I last saw him.'

'He's over the worst of that now,' Bill answered awkwardly.

'Can we get on, Logan?' his uncle snapped. 'I'm sure Mr Lane has a perfectly charming little boy——'

'Oh, he has,' Logan nodded.

'But he is hardly the reason for this meeting,' his uncle continued sharply.

'No, of course not,' Logan drawled mockingly. 'Carry on, Charles.'

'Thank you!'

'You're welcome,' he taunted.

To Callie the whole meeting had been turned into a farce. Bill had been angrily resentful towards Logan on her behalf, and with a few thoughtful words Logan had totally bemused the other man. It had been cleverly done; Logan had used every man's weakness towards his son to reduce Bill to just another indulgent father, not the important ally she had thought he would be.

She only half listened to the start of the meeting, finding all the technical talk boring in the extreme. She would certainly never make a business-woman!

'And now we come to the subject of expansion,' Sir Charles beamed at them all. 'I don't think there's any need to discuss it further, we all know how we're going to vote.'

'Callie?' Logan prompted.

'Yes,' she sighed. 'I'm ready.'

'So am I,' he nodded to his uncle.

'Would it be simpler to say who is for or who is against?' Sir Charles boomed.

Both Callie and Logan remained silent, and she could see the older man's confidence begin to waver.

'Caroline?' he questioned sharply.

'Finish the vote, Charles,' Logan instructed, his steady gaze never leaving Callie's face.

'But Caroline——'

'Against,' Logan said firmly.

'Against,' Callie echoed.

The reactions about her were instantaneous—Sir

Charles' voice raised in protest, Logan's smile of approval. She had known Sir Charles wouldn't like her decision, but she had known there was no other one she could make.

'I don't understand,' Sir Charles was babbling, taken completely by surprise. 'Caroline, you can't mean this!'

She stood up to leave. 'I do,' she said firmly. 'If you want to know why, I'm sure Bill will be only too glad to discuss it with you.'

'Of course.' Bill instantly recognised her cry for help.

'Sir Charles—Mr Carrington,' she nodded distantly to both of them, a coolly composed figure—on the outside at least—as she left the office and walked out to the lift.

She knew she looked very businesslike in her black suit and tan coloured blouse, a tan clutch-bag in her hand. And yet it was all a pose, below the knee-length skirt her legs were knocking together.

'Callie?'

Logan caught up with her as she stepped into the lift, pressing the button for the ground floor.

Callie was very conscious of him in the close proximity of the small lift, the way the dark grey suit was tailored on him, the cufflinks she had bought him in the cuffs of the white shirt he wore, his dark hair resting low down on his collar.

He turned to look at her. 'Why?'

She shrugged, making no effort to look as if she didn't know what he was talking about. 'It wouldn't have been in the company's best interests,' she said stiltedly, wondering if the lift was ever going to reach the ground floor.

'Very commendable,' he drawled. 'Now the real reason? I would have bet everything I have that you would side with Charles, just to spite me.'

'To spite you, yes.' Her eyes flashed, the moment of revelation upon her; this game had gone on long enough. 'But it wasn't what my stepfather wanted.' She looked at him with unwavering eyes as she saw him pale. 'No, Jeff wouldn't have approved of expanding Spencer Plastics. You told me that yourself, and for once I believe you.' She stepped out into the reception area and hurried towards the double glass doors, feeling as if her legs were made of stone, each step an effort.

CHAPTER NINE

LOGAN kept up with her step for step. 'Callie!' His hand was on her arm as they stepped out on to the pavement. 'For God's sake explain that last remark,' he demanded tautly.

She looked up at him with defiant eyes. 'It's quite simple, Logan. Contrary to what everyone thinks, Jeff was my stepfather, not my lover.'

He shook his head dazedly. 'I don't understand.'

'My mother was married to your uncle.' Another thought occurred to her. 'That makes me your step-cousin,' she said bitterly.

'But Charles was convinced Jeffrey was living with a woman called Caroline Day!'

'He was—my mother. And she wasn't Caroline Day when they lived together,' she hailed a passing taxi, hardly able to believe her luck when it actually stopped, 'she was Caroline Spencer,' she told Logan as she climbed into the back of the taxi.

'You can't go like this,' he frowned. 'I haven't finished talking to you.'

'There's nothing left to say.'

'Callie——'

'Where to, love?' the driver turned to ask.

'I——'

'Callie, I want to talk to you,' Logan said harshly.

'I have nothing else to say,' she told him distantly.

'But——'

'I can't wait here for ever, love,' the driver

interrupted a second time. 'I'm on a double yellow line.'

'Would you kindly stay out of this?' Logan snapped viciously.

'Pardon me for living,' the man mumbled as he turned back in his seat.

Logan shot him another impatient glance. 'Callie, get out of there and we can go somewhere and talk.'

'I told you, there's nothing to talk about.' She leant forward and gave the driver her address. 'Goodbye, Logan.' She gave him a cold look, and slammed the door in his face.

'Whew!' the driver chuckled as he moved the taxi out into the flow of traffic, glancing at Logan in his mirror. 'Bit of a fiery one, isn't he?'

'Yes,' she replied woodenly, not in the mood for conversation.

'Your husband?'

'No,' she shivered.

'Then he'll be back.' He winked at her in his driving mirror. 'He wouldn't want to lose a looker like you!'

An unwilling smile curved her lips. 'Thank you.'

But she knew Logan wouldn't be back, that in the circumstances she didn't want him back. Knowing Jeff was her stepfather might have changed things as far as Logan was concerned, but nothing had changed for her. Logan had used her; nothing could ever change that.

Marilyn invited her in for a cup of tea once she got back. 'I left poor Bill to cope with Sir Charles,' Callie explained ruefully.

'Don't worry,' her friend smiled. 'After the put-down he got from Sir Charles the first time around he's quite up to coping with him.'

'I hope so.' Callie sipped her tea, her hand trembling slightly—something Marilyn was quick to see.

'Was it rough?' she asked gently.

She grimaced. 'Not too bad.' Except that last scene with Logan. And strangely that had given her no satisfaction. She had thought she would feel elated when she told him her true relationship to Jeff, but in reality it had changed nothing between them.

'Was Sir Charles—Hey, was that your doorbell?' Marilyn frowned.

'I didn't hear anything . . .' she slowly replaced the cup in the saucer.

'When you have a baby as active as Paul you become aware of every noise,' Marilyn laughed. 'There it was again. No, don't move, I'll go.'

Callie had a terrible feeling, like Marilyn, that it was Logan. 'If it's him——'

'I'll tell him you aren't back yet.' Marilyn squeezed her arm reassuringly.

'Thanks.' She gave a grateful smile.

She should have known Marilyn wasn't strong enough to keep Logan out!

He marched into the room a couple of seconds later, a harassed-looking Marilyn following behind him. 'I want to talk to you, Callie,' he rasped without preliminary. 'Can we go to your flat, or would you rather talk here?'

Marilyn looked totally bemused. 'Oh, but——'

'Your flat?' Logan repeated harshly, with eyes only for Callie.

'If you insist,' she said stiffly, standing up. 'I'm sorry about this, Marilyn.'

Her friend shrugged acceptance of the situation. 'Just call if you need me.'

Logan's mouth tightened. 'I don't intend harming Callie, just talking to her.'

Marilyn returned his cold look in full measure. 'In the past you haven't seemed to know the difference.'

He drew in an angry breath. 'It's been mutual,' he ground out. 'Callie?' he prompted.

She led the way through to her flat, turning to face him as he closed the door behind them. 'What do you have to say?'

He sighed, shaking his head. 'You must have realised the shock you gave me this afternoon about my uncle. We none of us had any idea he'd married, that he had a stepdaughter.'

'That much has been obvious,' she scorned.

'How could we have any idea——'

'How could you *not*?' she snapped, her eyes flashing. 'He was a wonderful man, a man with principles—how could you believe him capable of living with a girl of my age? How could *you* believe I would live with a man old enough to be my father, Logan—unless, as I now know, the love you once professed for me was a lie.'

'*That*'s a lie!' he ground out. 'I still love you. Even when I believed you were my uncle's mistress I still loved you, still *love* you.'

The quiet intensity of his voice made her spin round. 'You don't know the meaning of the word!'

'I know I love you enough to want to marry you.' He met her angry gaze steadily.

'Me—and the Spencer shares,' she rasped, a bitter twist to her mouth.

'Damn the shares——'

'Damn them, Logan?' she scorned. 'When you were willing to go to such lengths to get them? Oh no, Logan, we won't damn them—at least, I won't. If it weren't for them I may never have met you. And if I hadn't met you I would never have known the disillusionment of trusting you with my love——'

'Callie——'

'Would you please leave,' she told him stiltedly. 'I never want to see you again.'

For a moment Logan looked as if he would continue the argument, then he sighed. 'All right, Callie, I'll go. But I'll be back, I promise you that.'

'If that means as much as the other promises you made me then I know I'll never see you again,' she scoffed, to hide the pain he wouldn't let die.

His eyes darkened. 'This promise is as sincere as the others I made you.' He pulled her into his arms, kissing her with unreserved passion, a dark flush to his cheeks when he at last released her. 'I love you, Callie. I hope one day I'll be able to make you believe that.'

'Maybe if you gave up your shares in Spencer Plastics,' she taunted.

'Or you gave up yours,' he said softly. 'Think about that, Callie.'

It took her several minutes after his departure to regain her composure, knowing that Marilyn would have heard Logan leave and would be curious about his reason for being here.

Bill was already home when she returned next door, looking none the worse for his talks with Sir Charles.

'How did it go?' she smiled.

'How do you think?' he said dryly. 'Sir Charles was absolutely furious about the way you voted. He seemed to think he could have expected more loyalty from his future daughter-in-law,' he added teasingly.

'He doesn't still believe that?' she gasped.

'He does,' Bill grinned. 'Some men never know when to accept defeat.'

'No . . .' Marilyn looked questioningly at Callie. 'Has Mr Carrington gone?'

Bill's eyes widened. 'He's been here?'

'Just now,' his wife nodded.

'I had a feeling he'd followed you, Callie.' He grimaced. 'Would I be speaking out of turn if I say I liked him?'

'Yes!'

'No,' Callie smiled at her friend's vehemence. 'He's a very likeable man.'

More than likeable, but she hoped she wouldn't have to see him again. Much as she hated to admit it, she had once again responded to his kisses.

She had a completely unexpected guest the next day—Cicely Carrington. Callie couldn't conceal her puzzlement when she saw the woman. Surely Logan hadn't involved his mother? Then she noticed the bandage on Cicely Carrington's left ankle. 'Logan didn't tell me you'd hurt your ankle,' she sighed her consternation. 'Please come in and sit down,' she invited without hesitation. Whatever reason the other woman had for being here, she liked her. 'Would you like a cup of tea?' she offered.

'Only if it's no trouble.' The elderly woman sank gratefully into a chair.

'Not at all,' and Callie escaped into the kitchen.

She had no idea why Cicely Carrington had come here today, but if, as she suspected, it was on Logan's behalf, then she didn't want to know. She liked the woman, but even so, Logan was a subject she didn't want to discuss with anyone.

But Mrs Carrington was in no hurry to get to the point of her visit, and accepted her cup of tea with one of her sweet smiles. 'This is a lovely flat,' she said warmly. 'Jeffrey was always very artistic—did he help decorate the flat?'

Callie smiled, remembering the fun they had had. Jeffrey might have been artistic, but when it came to practical things like wallpapering he was completely hopeless. She and her mother had been in hysterics by the time it was finished. Jeff had shut himself away in his studio for a week, to do 'some real work,' he said. It had been a standing joke in the family for months afterwards.

'Yes, he helped,' she told the other woman. 'Under protest. I'm afraid sculpture was his real art.'

'Yes, Logan told me how clever he was. Logan knows about these things,' she added without conceit for her son.

Callie remembered the way he had instantly recognised the work in the studio as being Thornton. 'Yes,' she acknowledged softly.

'I'm so sorry I haven't called earlier,' Mrs Carrington apologised as she accepted her cup of tea. 'It was so silly of me to fall over as I did.'

'I had no idea you'd hurt your ankle,' said Callie.

'Just a sprain, dear,' she confided. 'I bruised my ego more than myself. I'm always telling Logan how independent I am, then I go and do something like this!'

Callie had stiffened at the mention of Logan. 'It could have happened to anyone—even him,' she added hardly.

Mrs Carrington smiled. 'No, never Logan.'

She was probably right, things like falling over in the snow didn't happen to people like Logan. But she wished Mrs Carrington would get down to the purpose of this visit; it couldn't just be a social call.

'You're wondering why I'm here, aren't you?' the elderly lady smiled kindly.

'Well—yes.'

'Well, as I said earlier, I would have come before, but I haven't been out much since my fall. But something Logan told me when he got home yesterday compelled me to come and talk to you.'

'Really?' Callie said tightly.

'Yes. I was so pleased to know that Jeffrey finally married the woman he loved. When Logan introduced you to me on Christmas Day I thought you looked familiar, but it was the name that fooled me. It never used to be Day, you see. And I'm not very good on faces,' she gave Callie a vague look.

Callie was totally bemused by this incomprehensible speech. If she didn't know better she would have said Cicely Carrington had been drinking. Maybe she was high on pain-killers for her ankle? Whatever the reason, she wasn't making much sense.

'I see,' she humoured her.

'Yes.' The other woman obviously thought she knew exactly what she was talking about. 'After all, Callie Day is nothing like Caroline Addy, is it?'

'No.' Callie's interest sharpened at the mention of her mother's maiden name. Maybe Mrs Carrington wasn't talking nonsense after all.

The faded grey eyes were smiling kindly. 'The first time I saw you it was like going back twenty-five years.'

'It was?' she frowned.

'You don't have the faintest idea what I'm talking

about, do you?' Cicely Carrington realised.

'Er—no,' Callie admitted.

'Didn't your mother and Jeff ever tell you?'

She licked her lips nervously. 'Tell me what?'

'Oh dear,' the other woman sighed. 'I thought—Oh well, it's just one more black mark against the family. And goodness knows we have enough of those where you're concerned. One more isn't going to make a great deal of difference.'

Callie had butterflies in her stomach, sure that something momentous was going to be revealed to her. 'Could you—could you just tell me?' she requested huskily.

'But of course, my dear. It was what I came here for, after all. Twenty-five years ago, when my brother Jeffrey was just twenty, and your mother only eighteen, she was spurned by the family as a possible wife for Jeffrey.'

This information, so unexpected, hit Callie like a blow to the face. 'You're saying they knew each other before six years ago?' she choked.

The other woman nodded. 'Before you were even born.'

Callie sat down with a bump, very pale. 'I—Could you tell me it all—please?' she said jerkily.

'Would you like me to get you some fresh tea?' Mrs Carrington offered. 'I'm afraid this has all been rather a shock for you.'

Only because her mother and Jeff had never even hinted at knowing each other in the past. But it could explain the youthfulness of the sculpture, the way Jeff had been so determined to marry her mother this time, despite her illness.

She accepted the cup of tea from Cicely Carrington,

allowing her to fuss over her for several minutes before insisting she be told everything.

'None of the Spencer family come out of this in a good light, I'm afraid,' Mrs Carrington said regretfully. 'Not even Jeffrey. But he was very young, and our father was even more dominating than Charles.'

That was hard to imagine, but Callie prompted Mrs Carrington to tell her the rest.

'Your mother was a maid at my parents' house. I was already married and had Logan at the time. He would have been about ten, I suppose. I remember how he hero-worshipped Jeffrey.'

'He was the sort of man heroes are made of,' Callie said woodenly.

'Yes, he was.' Tears glistened in the faded grey eyes. 'I wish I'd known of his death in time to come to the funeral. Logan said he died very soon after your mother?'

'Three months.'

'How terrible for you!'

'Yes. My mother was the maid...?' Callie prompted.

'Oh yes. I'm sorry, my dear, my mind's not as active as it used to be. But I remember your mother well. She was a lot like you to look at, and always full of life and happiness. You may have realised that Jeffrey, Charles, and myself had a rather strict upbringing, with not too much love. Your mother brought sunshine into Jeffrey's life. He loved her from the first moment, and she loved him too.'

'What went wrong?'

'My father interfered,' Cicely sighed. 'We weren't so quick to defy our parents in those days, and Jeffrey was very young.'

'So he gave my mother up under family pressure,' Callie said disgustedly.

'It wasn't as simple as that.'

'But he did give her up?'

'Yes. You see, my father threatened him with disinheritance, with social ruin. A boy of twenty doesn't quite have his priorities sorted out properly. Your mother left my father's employ, and we never saw her again.'

'And Jeff?'

'He knew almost straight away that he'd made a mistake, but by that time your mother had disappeared.'

'Disgusted, I should think,' Callie derided bitterly. The whole thing sounded like some Victorian melodrama!

'She has hurt, very hurt, so hurt that she married the first man who showed her kindness and love.'

'I thought you said you never heard from her again?' Callie frowned.

'We didn't, but Jeffrey finally traced her. By that time she was married to Norman Day, and was expecting his child. She admitted to still loving Jeffrey, but her loyalty was to her husband and the child she was to give him. This time Jeffrey was the one to leave, swearing he would never trouble her life again. He made a life for himself, a lonely life, and he never forgot your mother.'

'It was all so cruel!' Callie choked.

Cicely Carrington sighed. 'My father was never a kind man. He pushed us all too hard, expected too much of us. Charles and I accepted it, Jeffrey never did. He was always the rebellious one. That night, after realising he had lost Caroline for good, he came back to the house, packed all his things and left. Our father swore he would disinherit him anyway. He was in such a temper because Jeffrey had thwarted him that he had a heart attack and died before he could change his will.'

Callie gave a cry of pain. 'Two people loving each other caused all that suffering?'

The other woman nodded emotionally. 'Jeffrey never accepted a penny of the money or his shares in the family business. He wanted nothing to do with us.'

'Can you blame him?'

'No. But I missed him.' Her voice trembled. 'Were they still very much in love?' She patted delicately at her cheeks with a silky handkerchief.

Callie could see how much her answer meant to the elderly woman, and she answered truthfully. 'Very much.' Her voice was husky.

So much was explained now—the way Jeff had come into their lives almost a year to the day after her father had died, claiming to be an old friend of his. Her mother hadn't wanted him in their home at first, but after a few weeks she had come to rely on the couple of evenings she allowed him to spend with her each week. Her mother had been happy with her father, she never doubted that, but with Jeff it had always been something special, with him her mother seemed to light up if he just entered a room. And it also explained the reason her mother had lived four and a half years when the doctors had given her a year at the most. Loving Jeff, finally being with him, had given her a reason to live.

'It's beautiful,' she choked, the tears falling unheeded.

'I think so,' the other woman nodded. 'I thought

you would like to share in their lifelong love, to let me tell you their story from the beginning.'

'Thank you.'

'Will you give my son the same chance to talk to you?' she asked gently.

'Logan?' Callie stiffened.

'It would be a pity to let history repeat itself.'

'I'm not a maid, to be browbeaten and discarded, and Logan certainly isn't an obedient young man of twenty!'

'He certainly isn't,' Cicely chuckled. 'And he wasn't. Logan has always had a mind of his own, it's the way we wanted him to be. He would never have given up your mother—as he doesn't want to lose you now.'

'We both agreed we should part, Mrs Carrington,' Callie said tautly. 'And nothing has happened to change my mind about that.'

'Logan wants you, no matter what he believes you to have done.'

'And what do you believe?' Callie stood up to pace the room. 'Do you also believe I deliberately set out to make him fall in love with me so that together we would have control of Spencer Plastics?'

'Certainly not!'

'You sound very sure.' Her mouth twisted.

'I am. I liked your mother, and I like you. And no matter what Logan may have said in the heat of the moment, he does love you. I can say with all honesty that I've seen my son in every mood possible, but never so disillusioned and hurt as he was on Christmas Day. I've never seen him drunk before either,' she grimaced. 'He spent the entire holiday period in a drunken haze. Not very good company at all!'

Callie had to smile at her expression of disgust. But her suspicions of Logan couldn't be dispelled so easily, she doubted they ever would be.

'It wouldn't work out,' she told his mother gently, knowing that Logan did still want her, but sure that the shares were a part of that want. 'We could never trust each other.'

'You're sure?' Cicely Carrington looked very disappointed.

'Very,' she nodded.

'Oh well.' The other woman stood up to leave. 'I've done my best. I did so hope you would be my daughter-in-law,' she said wistfully. 'Logan tells me Jeffrey had a studio here,' she added almost shyly. 'Do you think I might see it?'

'Of course!' Callie's agreement was instantaneous.

For the next half hour she showed Jeff's sister the extent of his skill, giving the other woman the figure of the elderly man, sure that Jeff would have wanted her to have it.

She returned to the studio once Cicely Carrington had left, picking up the sculpture of her mother. Oh, how she and Jeff must have loved each other, a love that had lasted over twenty years despite their not seeing each other. Would her love for Logan last as long, despite his duplicity?

CHAPTER TEN

THE telephone rang harshly in Callie's ear the next morning, waking her from what could only be described as a restless sleep, at worst hours of lying awake wondering what she was going to do. Once Jeff's will was finally settled she would have to take her partnership in Spencer Plastics a lot more seriously. And with Logan and Sir Charles against her she had formidable opponents.

She picked up the telephone, still groggy from her disturbed night.

'Miss Day?' She instantly recognised the crusty tones of James Seymour.

'Yes?' She was instantly wide awake.

'Would it be possible for you to come and see me immediately?'

She jack-knifed into a sitting position, with a feeling of foreboding. 'Is there anything wrong?'

'It's a very—private matter. Not something I would wish to discuss over the telephone,' he told her in his prim, unemotional voice.

Callie was already getting out of bed. 'What time would you like me to be there?'

'As soon as possible.'

Something was wrong, she knew it was. It usually took weeks to get an appointment with a lawyer, James Seymour wanted to see her immediately, this morning.

It had to be something to do with Jeff's will. Perhaps her fear had come true after all, perhaps there had been a mistake. If that were the case, would she be relieved or saddened? She had no idea how she would feel. And that might not be the reason James Seymour wanted to see her.

She wasted no more time thinking about it, washing and dressing in record time, then hurrying to James Seymour's office. When a man like him said it was urgent, then it was urgent. Callie was shown straight into his office.

Once again she was the focus of his disapproval as he looked over his gold-rimmed glasses at her casual trousers and top, the way her hair swung loosely about her shoulders, slightly ruffled by the cold breeze outside.

Callie ignored his critical gaze. 'You said you wanted to see me,' she prompted impatiently at his delay, just wanting to get this over with.

'Yes. I—— What I'm about to tell you is—well, it's rather difficult for me.'

She could tell by his evasive expression that it was something serious. 'The shares and money aren't mine after all,' she said dully. 'It's all a mistake, it belongs to someone else.'

His eyes widened. 'You already knew? Really, Miss Day, I must protest at your deception——'

'I didn't deceive anyone,' she sighed. 'I just knew it was too good to be true. Who do they really belong to?'

'Well, as Mr Spencer died intestate——'

'But there was a will—I saw it,' she frowned.

'Yes, there was a will,' James Seymour looked uncomfortable. 'But acting on information furnished to me by Mr Carrington——'

'Logan?' she echoed sharply.

'Just so,' the lawyer nodded. 'Mr Carrington learnt recently, two days ago to be precise, that his uncle married four years ago. I have in fact ascertained confirmation of the marriage since speaking to him.'

'Yes?'

'Mr Spencer's will was dated five years ago.'

'So?' she frowned.

'Any marriage revokes a will,' he explained. 'I take it you were not adopted by Mr Spencer?'

'Of course not,' she dismissed scathingly. 'I was already eighteen when they married.'

'As I thought,' he nodded. 'Mr Spencer should have informed me of his marriage and we could have drawn up a new will. In the circumstances——'

'It all reverts back to Sir Charles and Cicely,' she said numbly.

'I'm afraid so——' He seemed to hesitate. 'There is one other thing I think we should clear up.'

'Please do.'

'Mr Carrington informed me that your mother's name was the same as yours, Caroline Day, and so owing to Mr Spencer's single state at the time the will was drawn up, I think it would be only natural to assume that he intended his beneficiary to be your mother.'

It was logical, it made sense, and it was probably right. She stood up to leave. 'Thank you, Mr Seymour. I—— What else can I say?' she gave a helpless shrug.

'I'm sorry, Miss Day,' he did sound genuinely regretful. 'There is one thing to be grateful for.'

'Oh yes?'

The ghost of a smile lightened his features. 'Owing to the methodical slowness of the British legal system the money hadn't yet been awarded to you.'

'That's a bonus?'

'Well, at least you hadn't spent it!'

Callie felt sure it was the nearest to a joke James Seymour could get, and she returned his smile. 'There is that.' She shook his hand. 'Thank you for being so gentle with me.'

She walked out into the street, no longer a part owner of a prosperous business or a rich young woman. It would have been nice to have been rich, she would be a fool to think otherwise, but strangely she felt good to just be Callie Day once again. At least now no one could exploit her—she had nothing to exploit!

So much for Logan not wanting to lose her! He had done everything he could to make sure everything was taken away from her. Well now she would never have to see him again.

Once again she retreated to the peace of Jeff's studio, looking at the figure of her mother with new eyes. Jeff hadn't just shown her mother without pain as she had always believed, he had shown her as the young girl he loved, the young girl she had always appeared to him.

'Callie . . .'

She turned to see Logan walking towards her, also looking down at the sculpture of her mother, very dark and attractive, making her feel startling alive.

'She was very beautiful,' he said huskily. 'I can understand why my uncle loved her all his life, why he waited for her.'

Callie turned away. 'Why are you here? To gloat?' she scorned.

Logan's eyes were darkly brooding as he looked at her. 'I'm here to ask you something.'

Her mouth twisted, her voice brittle. 'If it's question and answer time you want, Logan, I'm not in the mood.'

'Only one question. Only one answer.'

She sighed. 'Well?'

'Will you marry me?'

Her head went back. 'What did you say?' she choked disbelievingly.

Logan grasped her upper arms, gazing deeply into her eyes, holding her captivated. 'Will you marry me?'

'Are you serious?' She searched the pale intensity of his face, seeing only anxiety written there.

'Never more so,' he said tautly.

'Why?'

'I thought it wasn't to be question and answer time,' he mocked. 'I've asked my question, I want the answer.'

'But——'

'Yes or no?'

Yes, she wanted to marry him, but no, she didn't want to be just another pawn in his game. But how could she be now, she no longer had the shares!

'I saw James Seymour this morning——'

'I know,' Logan nodded impatiently.

'He told you . . .?'

'Yes.'

'And you still want to marry me?'

'Oh yes,' he said with certainty. 'Why else do you think I had the problem of those shares removed? I knew you would never marry me while they stood between us.' His hand tightened. 'Now answer me, Callie.'

'But——'

'Yes or no?' he repeated hardly.

'Yes. But——'

'No buts, Callie,' he groaned, his arms tightly about her as he pulled her fully into his arms. 'No ifs or maybes either. I love you, I want to marry you—I'm *going* to marry you.'

'But it was all a trick on your part——'

'On the part of fate,' he corrected. 'I can see that now. I mocked my uncle with a remark that was never meant to be taken seriously, a remark I'd forgotten two minutes after saying it, and on Christmas Day it backfired on me. I taunted Charles with the idea that Donald should marry the woman Jeffrey had lived with if he wanted to keep the shares in the family. I've never had time for Spencer Plastics, only took control of my mother's shares to prevent Charles hounding her. As you may have gathered, Jeffrey kept pretty well out of any decisions concerning the business too.'

'Except when it came to expansion,' she reminded him.

'Yes,' he smiled. 'Charles will be able to go ahead with that now. And knowing his damned luck he'll make a success of it too! God, how he panicked at the thought of what he thought would be a money-grasping older woman coming into the business. He must have thanked his guardian angel when you turned up. Hell, I didn't even know the name of the woman he was so up in arms about, I simply wasn't interested enough to find out. I was shocked out of my mind on Christmas Day when I found *you* were that woman.'

'But I wasn't, my mother was married to Jeff.' Callie was snuggled in his arms, loving each wonderful word of his explanation.

'How could we know that, Jeffrey certainly never

told anyone. If James Seymour could make that mistake, how could us lesser mortals know any better?' he taunted.

She giggled. 'Mr Seymour doesn't like you either.'

'I know,' he chuckled. 'We were meant to meet,' he said earnestly. 'Can't you see that, Callie? We were meant to meet and fall in love.'

'Oh yes!' She could only believe him now, knew that she had nothing but herself that he might want. His love hadn't been a deception at all, but a wonderful reality, a reality that had almost been destroyed because of their distrust of each other.

'I have another piece of news that might interest you,' he murmured after kissing her thoroughly.

'Yes?' she said dreamily.

'Donald has eloped, with Lena McDonnell!'

'Donald . . .? My goodness,' she couldn't help laughing. 'Lena . . .?' she said slowly. 'Don't I know that name?'

'Let's go through to the drawing-room and make ourselves comfortable, then I'll tell you everything.' He settled her into the curve of his arm as they sat side by side on the sofa. 'Lena is—was, Charles's secretary.'

A memory of the busty blonde with hard blue eyes came to mind. 'Oh dear! Poor Donald!'

'Oh, I don't know,' Logan lightly kissed her temple.

'Don't you indeed?' Jealousy ripped through her. How could she have possibly thought she could go through life without this man?

'Not in that way, darling,' his arms tightened about her. 'I meant that Lena will be able to stand up to Charles and Susan, something Donald could never do on his own. Lena is made of sterner stuff.'

'But won't your uncle disinherit him?'

'And risk it all coming to me?' he taunted. 'Oh no, he'll forgive Donald. He'll even accept Lena as his wife, especially when the grandchildren come along.'

Callie giggled. 'I can't imagine Donald as a father!'

'How about me?'

'Oh yes. I——' she broke off, blushing. 'Well——'

'It's all over, Callie, the whole nightmare.' Logan kissed her fiercely on the mouth. 'And it has been a nightmare.'

'Your mother said you've been drinking.'

'Mm,' he grimaced. 'I couldn't believe the woman I loved, the woman you were, could do something like that. And yet on the evidence I had, it appeared there could be no other explanation.'

'For me too.'

'When you told me two days ago that Jeffrey had been your stepfather, and that your mother's name had been the same as yours, I began to hope. I put my idea to Seymour, knowing it was my last chance with you. Thank God it paid off!' he shuddered.

'And if it hadn't?'

'I would have kept trying anyway. Once I got over the initial shock I still wanted to marry you.'

'And Audrey?'

'Has walked out on me,' he told her ruefully.

'She has?' Callie burst out laughing.

'Mm. She took exception to the attention I paid to you on New Year's Eve, said I had just been using her. Which was true. I couldn't even look at another woman, let alone want to make love to one. I couldn't get you out of my mind, couldn't stay away from you.'

'You've been very insulting.'

'I was hurt, Callie.' He looked deeply into her eyes,

his love shining there for her to see. 'I fell almost instantly in love with you, thought you felt the same way——'

'I do!'

'It didn't seem that way. After all, you'd never mentioned the money or the shares to me.'

She chewed on her bottom lip, searching for the right words to explain her feelings. 'You have to understand, inheriting those things was like winning the football pools, something you only ever dream about but never think will really happen to you. I had a feeling from the beginning that it couldn't really be true. And I was right.'

'Oh, darling, I'm so sorry,' Logan sighed. 'But I have something else you can do with your life if you're interested,' he added teasingly.

'Being your secretary?'

'No, I've already replaced Audrey.'

'Oh?'

'With a competent woman of fifty.'

'Some of these older women——'

'Not this one,' he laughed. 'Mrs Taylor does a good impression of a sergeant-major inspecting her troops. I'm terrified of her.'

'Oh, good,' said Callie with satisfaction. 'Now what do you think I should do with my life?'

'I think you should let me marry you, let me worship you. Be the mother of my children. Callie, I love you, and I need you so badly. This last week without you has been——'

Her fingertips on his lips stopped further conversation. 'I need you too. I thought my heart would break when we parted the way we did. I know you don't like me to talk about Jeff, but——'

'Only when I thought you'd loved him before loving me. I'm very possessive where you're concerned. So talk away, darling. He sounds like a man I would have admired.'

'I'm sure of it,' she nodded fervently. 'And he would have liked you too. He would have approved of our being married, of our loving each other.'

'My love for you is as strong as his was for your mother. Stronger,' Logan vowed. 'I'll love you for a lifetime too.'

And Callie knew he would, knew that she would always be safe in his love.

Harlequin Plus
A CLASSIC LOVE STORY

When Callie escapes from the hubbub of the party to the quiet privacy of the library, she pulls from the bookshelf her favorite romantic novel, *Jane Eyre*. Written by Charlotte Brontë and published in England in 1847, it is considered a classic of English literature—and an early model for the popular Harlequin romances of today!

In Brontë's novel, Jane is a poor but independent orphan who takes a position as a governess to a young child at a great mansion called Thornfield. Her employer is the handsome Edward Rochester, a solemn and moody individual, who is distant and rather brusque toward Jane. Nevertheless she is strangely attracted to him. Eventually Rochester comes to admire Jane's stubborn determination, plucky independence and resolute cheerfulness. He falls in love with her and proposes marriage. But at their wedding, it is disclosed that he already has a wife—who for many years has been completely insane. Worse, Jane learns that the woman inhabits several rooms on the third floor of Rochester's mansion! Humiliated, and refusing Rochester's offer to be his mistress, Jane leaves Thornfield forever.

One night, far away in another part of England, Jane hears Rochester calling to her in a dream. She rushes back to find Thornfield a burned and blackened ruin, deliberately set afire by the mad wife, and Rochester himself blinded when he tried unsuccessfully to rescue the unfortunate woman from the flames. Reunited at last and free from his terrible past, Rochester and Jane marry. Two years later, with the birth of their first child, Edward regains the sight of one eye.

The moving and dramatic story of *Jane Eyre* has been read and loved by millions of women the world over. Readers cannot help but admire Charlotte Brontë's heroine for her independence and strength—the same qualities they admire in modern-day heroines like Carole Mortimer's Callie Day!

Readers rave about Harlequin romance fiction...

"I absolutely adore Harlequin romances! They are fun and relaxing to read, and each book provides a wonderful escape."
—N.E.,* Pacific Palisades, California

"Harlequin is the best in romantic reading."
—K.G., Philadelphia, Pennsylvania

"Harlequin romances give me a whole new outlook on life."
—S.P., Mecosta, Michigan

"My praise for the warmth and adventure your books bring into my life."
—D.F., Hicksville, New York

*Names available on request.

ALL-TIME FAVORITE BESTSELLERS
...love stories that grow more beautiful with time!

Now's your chance to discover the earlier great books in Harlequin Presents, the world's most popular romance-fiction series.

Choose from the following list.

FAV-CB-2

ALL-TIME FAVORITE BESTSELLERS

Complete and mail this coupon today!

Harlequin Reader Service

In the U.S.A.
1440 South Priest Drive
Tempe, AZ 85281

In Canada
649 Ontario Street
Stratford, Ontario N5A 6W2

Please send me the following Presents **ALL-TIME FAVORITE BESTSELLERS.** I am enclosing my check or money order for $1.75 for each copy ordered, plus 75¢ to cover postage and handling.

☐ #17	☐ #35	☐ #41	☐ #66	☐ #73
☐ #20	☐ #36	☐ #42	☐ #67	☐ #75
☐ #29	☐ #38	☐ #50	☐ #70	☐ #78
☐ #32	☐ #39	☐ #62	☐ #71	

Number of copies checked @ $1.75 each = $ _____
N.Y. and Ariz. residents add appropriate sales tax $ _____
Postage and handling $ .75
                    TOTAL $ _____

I enclose _____
(Please send check or money order. We cannot be responsible for cash sent through the mail.)
Prices subject to change without notice.

NAME _____
                    (Please Print)

ADDRESS _____ APT. NO. _____

CITY _____

STATE/PROV. _____

ZIP/POSTAL CODE _____

Offer expires November 30, 1983   30556000000

Take these 4 best-selling novels FREE

Yes! Four sophisticated, contemporary love stories by four world-famous authors of romance FREE, as your introduction to the Harlequin Presents subscription plan. Thrill to **Anne Mather**'s passionate story BORN OUT OF LOVE, set in the Caribbean.... Travel to darkest Africa in **Violet Winspear**'s TIME OF THE TEMPTRESS.... Let **Charlotte Lamb** take you to the fascinating world of London's Fleet Street in MAN'S WORLD.... Discover beautiful Greece in **Sally Wentworth**'s moving romance SAY HELLO TO YESTERDAY.

Harlequin Presents...

The very finest in romance fiction

Join the millions of avid Harlequin readers all over the world who delight in the magic of a really exciting novel. EIGHT great NEW titles published EACH MONTH! Each month you will get to know exciting, interesting, true-to-life people .... You'll be swept to distant lands you've dreamed of visiting .... Intrigue, adventure, romance, and the destiny of many lives will thrill you through each Harlequin Presents novel.

Get all the latest books before they're sold out!
As a Harlequin subscriber you actually receive your personal copies of the latest Presents novels immediately after they come off the press, so you're sure of getting all 8 each month.

Cancel your subscription whenever you wish!
You don't have to buy any minimum number of books. Whenever you decide to stop your subscription just let us know and we'll cancel all further shipments.